*Commander Kellie and the Superkids*_{SM}

#10

The Runaway Mission

Christopher P.N. Maselli

KENNETH
COPELAND
PUBLICATIONS

Unless otherwise noted, all scripture is from the following translations: *The Holy Bible, New International Version*, ©1973, 1978, 1984 by the International Bible Society. Used by permission of Zondervan Publishing House.

International Children's Bible, New Century Version, ©1986, 1988 by Word Publishing, Dallas, Texas 75039. Used by permission.

Commander Kellie and the Superkids$_{SM}$ is a registered servicemark of Heirborne$_{TM}$.

Based on the characters created by Kellie Copeland Kutz, Win Kutz, Susan Wehlacz and Loren Johnson.

The Runaway Mission

ISBN 1-57562-805-8   30-0910

09 08 07 06 05 04   6 5 4 3 2 1

©2004 Eagle Mountain International Church, Incorporated
aka Kenneth Copeland Publications

Kenneth Copeland Publications
Fort Worth, Texas 76192-0001

For more information about Kenneth Copeland Ministries, call 1-800-600-7395 or visit www.kcm.org.

To Elizabeth Stewart and Jenny VanWagner for bringing alive two of the most enjoyable characters to write...

Contents

Dear Superkid,

I'm Valerie Rivera, and I recently had to face some hard truths. There I was, listening to our next assignment from Commander Kellie when—wow!—all of a sudden I was somewhere else...somewhere I wasn't sure I wanted to be.

If you don't already know, I'm a member of the Blue Squad at Superkid Academy. The Blue Squad consists of me and my friends: Paul, Missy, Rapper, Alex and Techno the robot. Of course, Commander Kellie is our leader. One of our team's main functions, other than daily training together, is going on assignment to help others. We usually go as a team with a plan and plenty of preparation—but not this time! This time I started out by myself with no plan, let alone any time to prepare.

But I knew God would bring me through in victory. All I had to do was rely on the power of hope. Then I had to help others do the same—which was the real challenge.

So how about it? Are you ready to see what God can do with an ordinary kid? If you are, let's get going and you'll see—hope will come alive in you!

                                          Valerie

The Runaway Mission

Lincoln could hear his mother weeping in the living room. Something else had happened, he knew it. It was that kind of weeping.

It was the same way she wept that night six months ago when his father died suddenly of a heart attack. The medics came quickly. Lincoln's mom—a nurse herself—tried everything she knew, but he couldn't be revived. The doctor explained that since it happened before she or Lincoln returned home, it was just too late.

The weeping was the same as Lincoln had heard three months ago, too, the last night he and his mother were in their house. She had tried to explain to him, without shedding a tear, that they had no insurance and that she couldn't afford to support them both—and stay in the house—on just her paycheck. But Lincoln could tell it was tearing her up inside.

Tonight, he could hear the weeping from his bedroom. It was a quiet murmur...a shaky breathing...and once in a while, a telltale squeak. Something had happened again, Lincoln just knew it.

He turned over in bed and faced the wall. By the glow of his night light, he could see the paint peeling. No matter how many times they called this place home, it would *never* be home. This was just a temporary residence. A low-cost apartment in a bad section of town. With any hope, they would leave soon. He had been praying about it every night, but he was starting to feel weary. And it had been months since he had heard his mother pray.

Saltwater crept into Lincoln's coal-colored eyes, blurring his vision. He blinked it away. He knew if his dad were there, he'd know what to do. Thoughts of his dad made Lincoln sit up in bed. He glared out of his bedroom door at the gentle light coming from the living room.

Lincoln didn't like it, but he had to be the dad now. He had to be the one to help his mom. He couldn't be like the 11-year-olds at his school anymore, spending hours playing video games and watching television. He didn't have time for those things.

Lincoln sat up in bed and grabbed his Bible. He flipped through it slowly, seeing text fly by that he'd read many times. He placed the Bible back on his nightstand, then shifted out of bed and shuffled to his doorway. The air held the chill of the wintry weather outside. After a pause for a deep breath, he proceeded to the living room.

His mom was sitting on the floor in front of the couch, clutching a framed picture. Lincoln stopped and shifted his feet. His mother looked up, startled. She quickly placed the picture on the coffee table and patted down her face with her palms, wiping her eyes dry as fast as she could. She sniffled.

"L!" she exclaimed, using his nickname as her voice broke. "What are you doing up? You have to get plenty of sleep so you'll be ready for school." Her forced smile kept trying to pull itself down into a frown.

L shook his head, looking down. "I don't like this school," he muttered. "I don't know anyone there." He tromped over to the couch and sat down. His mother, sitting on the floor in front of him, leaned back, resting on his legs. Lincoln brushed her short, dark hair with his fingers. Six months ago, he never would have imagined he would be sitting there consoling his mother.

"What's wrong, Mom?" Lincoln whispered. His mother shook her head, not turning to look at him.

"No matter what happens, promise me you'll be all right."

L swallowed hard. "Mom, wha…"

His mother grabbed the hand stroking her hair. *"Promise me, Lincoln."*

L nodded his head. "Yeah, Mom…I promise."

She tapped his hand. "Go ahead and go to bed, L. Tomorrow's another day."

Lincoln nodded again. His mom leaned forward as he stood. He looked down at the picture sitting on the coffee table. It was the last one taken of his dad, his mom and L together. They were all dressed in their Sunday best, smiling widely. It had been a long time since either L or his mom had smiled like that.

But tomorrow *would* be another day.

✪ ✪ ✪

Lincoln woke up late the next day as the sunlight filtered into his room through bent miniblinds. He hopped out of bed anxiously; he didn't like being late for school. The water he showered under was lukewarm at best, but he was beginning to get used to it.

Exiting the shower, he tied his towel around his waist, grabbed his toothbrush and started brushing. The strong, cleansing mint lightly burned his mouth, but it felt good. He opened the bathroom door and called his mother's name. No answer came. He called again. Still no answer.

L blinked and thought for a moment, then spit out his mouthful of toothpaste bubbles. A small ring still surrounded his lips, but he didn't pay any attention. He walked into the living room, his toothbrush still in hand.

The lights were all off, but otherwise the room was just as he and his mother had left it the night before. The gloom of sorrow still hung in the air. L noticed the picture frame on the coffee table was facedown. He walked over and set it straight up. Some money was underneath it, which Lincoln thought was rather strange.

"Mom?" he called out again. Nothing. He went straight to her bedroom. Her bed was made. L wondered if it had been slept in. Something about it all seemed so odd. Perhaps she had been called away to the retirement home where she worked. *Yes,* he thought, *that was probably it.*

L finished brushing his teeth and got dressed. He thought about grabbing his Bible for morning devotions, but decided to pass. He had too much on his mind.

He ate a breakfast of cereal and milk. Even though the milk smelled slightly sour, it tasted OK. Minutes later, he ran out the door, throwing on his jacket and backpack as he left. He knew he'd just barely make the bus. Then when he came back that afternoon, he would see his mother and ask what had happened to call her away.

❂　❂　❂

Lincoln ate dinner alone—a warmed-up bowl of beans and franks. Not exactly gourmet, but filling. He often looked at the clock wondering when his mother would return from her long shift.

L didn't mind being alone. He had felt alone more than ever lately. But he didn't like being alone in a building where he couldn't trust anyone. It was no comfort to know that across the hall lived the big, angry landlord, who owned an old-fashioned shotgun—and liked showing off with it. L remembered that man holding the gun as he challenged L's mom about the rent—saying she hadn't paid when she had. Sometimes he even accused the two of them, saying they didn't belong on the premises...which was about the only thing that crazed, old man was right about.

L stayed up as late as he could, but fell asleep on the sofa.

After three days of the same, the reality of the situation settled on Lincoln. He realized his mother had left. She wasn't at work. She was gone. That meant he might be at home alone for awhile. But eventually, surely, his mother would come back.

He sat on the couch, staring at the picture of himself, his mom and his dad. He remembered when the picture was taken, how they laughed at the silly jokes the photographer told. Their laughter sounded like music.

L prayed, *God, please bring my mom back and make everything right.* He couldn't think of anything else to say. A thought entered his mind, and he wondered if God was even listening. After all, it had been so long since L had heard any music.

Ten more long days passed. Then one afternoon Lincoln was startled by a knock at the door. He hadn't had any visitors and, quite frankly, he was happy about that. He wasn't sure what he'd say to them if they started asking questions. Besides, he was doing fine. He still had a little bit of money left that he hadn't spent on groceries, and he hadn't missed one day of school.

The knock came again. Lincoln decided it would be better to answer the door than to arouse suspicion. L stood on his tiptoes and peeked through the peephole. It was Ms. Skinner, his school principal. *Great.*

Lincoln decided to act as easygoing as possible. Maybe she was just here for a friendly visit. *Yeah, right.*

L opened the door. Ms. Skinner's smile made it worth opening.

"Hello, Lincoln," she said in her middle-aged, Southern dialect. L liked the way her vowels stretched when she talked. Her graying, dark hair was in a bun, accenting her dark, round face. "How are you doing this afternoon?"

"I'm fine." L didn't elaborate.

"May I come in?"

"It's not very clean."

The door across the hall opened and the man with the shotgun peered through the crack.

"That's all right," she said, inviting herself into the apartment. L stepped aside and allowed her entrance. The man across the way closed his door.

"Lincoln, where's your mother?"

Lincoln winced more noticeably than he had wanted. *Why did she have to ask that?*

"She's out," he said, trying not to lie too badly.

"Out where?" Ms. Skinner asked, walking around the apartment, craning her neck as she peeked into the bedrooms.

"Just out," L stated.

Ms. Skinner stopped looking around and walked over to L. She crouched down, facing him eye to eye.

"Lincoln, you can tell me the truth."

"What do you mean?" L asked.

"Your teacher told me your grades are dropping, you're not talking much to the other kids, and you've been trading trinkets for other kids' sack lunches at school."

L remained solid.

"Lincoln, I've been working in this school system for 23 years. I know what to look for, and I know what this part of town is like. Now, I can help you, but you have to tell me the truth."

"She's coming back," L said defensively.

Ms. Skinner answered, "I know she is."

"I'm doing fine. I can survive until she returns."

"When did she leave?"

L shrugged, giving in. "About two weeks ago."

Ms. Skinner nodded sadly. That was it. No orders, no more questions, just a nod. She walked over to the phone and dialed a number. L wished they still had the ComPhone they used to have. Then he could see the person she was talking to on the view screen. But they had to sell it and all they could afford was "the old kind" of phone with a hand-held receiver.

ComPhone or not, it didn't take L long to figure out that Ms. Skinner was calling social services. She was using hushed tones, but she wasn't quiet enough. L frowned. What if they came and took him away from the apartment? What if they forced him to live somewhere far away where his mom couldn't find him? What if he had to live with people he didn't know...or even *want* to know?

As she talked, Lincoln stepped quietly over to the coffee table. He picked up the picture frame and the remaining money beside it. Swiftly, he grabbed his thick jacket and backpack off a chair in the kitchen. And, when Ms. Skinner's back was toward him, he slipped out the door.

✪ ✪ ✪

Two months passed, and L never returned to the apartment. He feared doing so might alert the authorities. He didn't want to be taken away—too far away for his mother to find. Instead, he lay low, on the streets, becoming accustomed to their ways, comforted in the fact that this part of town was too seedy for anyone to even care about a misplaced kid. He spent the nights at an old, local mission. During the day he wandered the streets, keeping his eyes wide-open for his mother to return, looking for him.

As he wandered, he kept his mouth shut. He refused to pray. Not even once. He figured there was no use. God obviously wasn't listening.

Or so he thought.

Valerie suddenly found herself freezing. Not just her fingers and toes, but her whole body felt like it had been instantly crammed into a tiny icebox. She blinked, but couldn't see anything. Breathing had quickly become difficult and she could barely move. She was stuck in…something.

Valerie forced herself to try and make sense of it. A split second ago she had been with the other Superkids, talking to Commander Kellie about their next mission—Valerie was certain. Commander Kellie had been filling them in on the details about a young boy named Lincoln Furlong who had run away. It was their mission to find him. Then Valerie blinked and everything instantly changed—no mission brief-ing, no Superkid Academy, no Commander Kellie, no Superkids...nothing but darkness and cold all around.

Valerie wondered: Had she fainted? Was she dreaming? Was this some kind of elaborate trick by NME, Superkid Academy's rival?

Valerie tried to shout out for help, but her voice emerged as just a low moan. What was happening to her? She felt mentally alert, but the confusing, crammed surroundings made her wonder.

She managed to squeeze her right hand and a cold, sandy substance crunched between her palm and fingers.

Abruptly, she heard a thump. Then another. And another. Lots of thumps. Everywhere. The icebox surrounding her vibrated as if it were alive. Then it stopped.

The next thing she heard was unmistakable. It was faint, like a drum. It was a bark—a dog's bark. If she hadn't grown up on Calypso Island with two dogs of her own, she might never have recognized the sound. It sounded just like her own dogs sounded when she was swimming...more precisely, when she was underwater.

But she *couldn't* be underwater now—how could that be possible? She could breathe! Barely, but she could!

Valerie squeezed her hand again. She felt the gritty substance slide between her fingers.

That's it, she thought. She was underground. *Buried* underground.

No—wait—she was freezing. She was under *snow.*

With that sudden realization, Valerie began to kick and dig with the little energy she could muster, momentarily wondering which way was up.

Suddenly her hand broke into the open air and a biting wind smacked it. Then a wet, warm, spongy something slapped it, like a slimy fish sliding across her palm. Valerie guessed that the wet, warm, spongy something must lead up and out of the icebox. She kicked and dug some more, pushing up with her face.

At once, her head broke through the crest of a snowdrift. Like a barrage of needles, sharp wind shot at her eyes and she closed them in reflex. She looked down at the piled snow and pushed herself the rest of the way out of the drift. Dancing snow glistened in the streetlight underneath the cloudy, nighttime sky. The dog she had heard was there—a small, awkward mix of poodle/cocker spaniel/Chihuahua. It licked her hand again with its long, slobbery, fishlike tongue.

"G-good boy," she whispered.

Valerie's hair dropped in front of her brown eyes. The dark-brown strands were clumped together, caked with snow crystals. As she pushed herself into a wobbly stance, she discovered she was wearing rags—torn, brown corduroy pants and a thick, green sweater. The brown shoes and dirty, white socks were equally ugly. Part of her felt like crying—not because of how she looked, but because she didn't understand.

"Father God," she whispered, "this doesn't make any sense to me, but I know You can fill me with wisdom and understanding. I pray that I have the mind of Christ right now." The prayer from Colossians 1:9 and 1 Corinthians 2:16 comforted her. Pulling encouragement around herself like a thick blanket, Valerie folded her arms across her chest and shivered.

The dog barked again, wagging its tail. Valerie looked around, but didn't recognize the area. Most of the buildings were closed or condemned. Footprints in the snow filled the street, like a stampede of people had run through the area. She assumed that was probably the thumping sound she had heard. The dog barked a third time.

As the wind continued to rip at her exposed face, Valerie realized her clothes were barely wet. She hadn't been under the snow for long. It just didn't make any sense.

"Snicker!" shouted a voice behind her. Valerie whirled around, half thankful she wasn't alone, half hoping the caller was friendly. From around the corner of a building, a young boy appeared dressed in dirty, dark jeans, an equally filthy, thick jacket and an old backpack. He stopped in his tracks when he saw Valerie standing there, staring at him. His eyes, the color of coal, were partially hidden beneath his falling, jet-black hair. His face showed his Asian descent.

The boy, who looked at least every one of Valerie's 11 years, peered down at the snowdrift. "Hey," he said, wrinkling his eyebrows. "Where'd you come from? Were you…under the snow?"

Valerie twisted her head and Snicker barked. She shivered again. "I…uh, think so." She felt very disoriented. "Your dog licked my hand and helped me find my way out."

"He likes stuff that shines," the boy said. "He must have seen your wet hand sticking out."

A short silence prevailed, then the boy looked down the street. He came forward, pressing into the cold wind, and picked up the mutt. "Haven't seen you out here before," he said to Valerie. She noticed him shiver, too.

"Can you tell me what I'm doing here?" the Superkid asked. A sudden gust whipped snowflakes against their reddened faces.

The boy turned. "C'mon. It's freezing. Let's get to the shelter. You'll be all right." He grabbed Valerie's arm. "I think we lost the raiders. But if I'm wrong, you don't want to be out here—especially on a night like this."

✪ ✪ ✪

Like a heavy cloud, hopelessness hovered over the crowd making its way into the sole, downtown shelter. Homeless men and women pushed their way in, out of the cold. Needle-sharp winds and dense snow sent shivering through the crowd, but no one complained. They each waited their turn.

Valerie, the boy and his dog, Snicker, took their place at the back of the line. The surrounding old buildings were all dark, like they belonged in an Old West ghost town. As Valerie relaxed and figured God had brought her there for a reason, her head cleared. She looked around and was surprised that even the homeless lived in a place so desolate. This small shelter was a lone star in the dark universe of inner-city streets.

Some faces were young, others old. Almost all of them were wrinkled in some way, if not with age, then with worry or sadness. Despite the cold, Valerie felt her heart expand with compassion. These were the lost, the lowly, the sick and the hurting. These were the type of people Valerie's missionary parents shared the gospel with as Valerie grew up on Calypso Island.

One old man, his skin thick and leathery, rolled forward through the snow in his old-fashioned wheelchair. Another, this one a woman, squeezed her shivering friend's shoulder. Still another coughed from deep in his lungs, sounding hoarse and sickly.

It seemed so wrong that anyone should have to live like they did—waiting for shelter, waiting for medical help, waiting for love. Valerie could almost envision herself standing up on a box and shouting to them, "There is hope! The only hope anyone has is in Jesus! Let me help you! Let *Him* help you!"

For now, until she found out where she was and what was going on, she decided it would be best for her to simply pray silently for them. At the same time, she committed in her heart that she would do more when she could.

It felt as though nearly an eternity passed before they finally reached the front door. Valerie noticed the sign on the window:

Welcome to
Geofferson Mission
Reverend Michael Bankson
Lodging 8 p.m.-8 a.m.

"I'm in Geofferson?" Valerie asked her new friend who was shoving the dog into his backpack. He nodded.

"I really am far from home," she added. The boy didn't seem interested. As they walked through the doors, he pointed to a wide room stemming off the lobby. It looked similar to the lobby itself—whitewashed walls and speckled white tile—but it had about 30 oak-stained pews inside.

"We'll go inside in a sec," he said. Then he explained, "We have to go listen in order to get a bed for the night." Valerie nodded, not totally understanding.

The boy crept down a side hallway and popped open a door. He looked around sneakily and then removed the canine from his backpack. *"Shhhh,"* he said to the mutt. Then he put him down in the room. As he began to close the door, the dog suddenly darted out.

"Snicker!" the boy scolded in a hushed voice. The mutt just stood there and wagged his tail. "If you don't get in there, they'll find you and put you outside for the night! Now, get in there!"

Wag, wag, wag.

The boy reached down for the dog. He dodged the boy's hands. Wag, wag, wag.

The boy motioned his hand to Valerie. "Hey, you have anything shiny?"

Not thinking much of it, Valerie looked around. She could feel her ears burning as they warmed. Snow was melting in her hair, surely making her look like she had just gotten out of a swimming pool.

Across the way, next to a large painting, Valerie spied a bulletin board. Blue crepe paper was twisted around the edges and the background was covered in white. Hanging along the sides, top and bottom were pairs of fake, rubber hands. In the middle, written in cut-out foil letters, was the message:

GIVE A HELPING HAND
SUPPORT
GEOFFERSON MISSION

Corny, but it got the point across. There was also a job listing. They needed a cook, a nurse, a janitor, an administrator... *They pretty much need a whole staff,* Valerie thought. She pulled the foil letter "A" off the board and walked it over to the boy. The dog followed the "A" every step of the way. Wag, wag, wag. The boy smiled, crumpled the letter into a ball and tossed it into the room. Snicker excitedly ran after it. The boy closed the door.

"Thanks," he said. "I guess now I owe them an 'A.'"

Valerie smiled. "Is there a ComPhone I can…"

"We have to go listen first," the boy interrupted, leading Valerie to the chapel. "That's the way it works. Listen to the dumb sermon, stay out of the cold. It's no fun, but it's worth it."

Valerie was going to challenge the boy's attitude, but he didn't give her the chance.

"My name's Lincoln," he said, not offering his hand to shake. "My friends call me L. Then again, I haven't seen any friends for a while."

Valerie stopped in her tracks. "Lincoln?" she asked. "Lincoln *Furlong?"*

That made L stop in his tracks. "Maybe. Why?"

Valerie's eyes widened. "Last thing I remember, I was getting ready to go on a mission to find you. I know your mother is missing, too."

"Who are you?" L retorted, backing up. "Some kind of secret, Social Services agent? I'm not leaving. She's coming back!"

"No, I just want to help," Valerie said, holding up her hands in surrender. "Please, let me help. My name's Valerie Rivera. I'm a Superkid."

L dropped his jaw in surprise. "A Superkid?" Then he smirked and said, "Yeah, right. And I'm *Wichita Slim.*"

Valerie looked down at the rags she was wearing. She pulled on a handful of her straight hair. "I know I don't look like one, but it's true. This doesn't make a lot of sense to me yet, either, but I do know I want to help."

"Fine," L said, surprising Valerie. "How are you gonna help?"

"Well, I've found you," she said. "What do you say we find your mother?"

Sitting in one of the homeless shelter's pews was as comfortable as sitting on a stone step. Valerie frequently found herself shifting positions to stay at ease. She wanted to call Commander Kellie, but the service had started and the ComPhone had been shut down. She'd just have to wait until afterward.

Despite the fact that most of the people in the room didn't look happy to be there, the homeless shelter chapel looked like a little church. The pews were filled with people. All of them were older than L and Valerie, but none seemed surprised to see them there.

At the front of the room, there was a podium with a big, white cross nailed to it. Behind it, the preacher, presumably the Reverend Michael Bankson, spoke lovingly yet forcefully. He was a lanky, middle-aged man, with thinning, brown hair and a big mustache. He also wore glasses—a commodity almost unheard of in this day and time. With the current setting, however, the glasses fit in perfectly. The whole room was like a vision out of the past, pulled into the present.

The preacher was saying, "As Luke 15 records, a son broke his relationship with his father. He left for a faraway country, to live how he pleased—and he took his inheritance with him."

Valerie noticed that L folded his arms across his chest.

The preacher added, "He partied and lived in sin, and

eventually he blew every last bit of money his father had given him. Out of cash, he ended up eating pig food to stay alive."

L rolled his eyes.

"What? You don't believe this story?" Valerie whispered to L. He shrugged.

"That's when the son realized he had everything—but only when he was with his father," the preacher continued. "So he decided to go home. *Perhaps,* he thought, *my father will at least let me work as his servant.*"

"I love this story," Valerie offered with another whisper. "It has a great ending."

"While the son was still a long way off, his father saw him coming. He got so excited that his son had returned, he ran up to him and hugged him tightly. The son was sorry and asked if he could start working for his father as a servant. 'No!' his father shouted. 'Bring the best clothes and cook up a great meal! For my son is alive again! He was lost and now is found!'"

"Yeah, yeah, yeah," L whispered.

"What makes you so cynical?" Valerie challenged.

"I hear this same story every night," L shot back. "But the preacher doesn't understand real life. He doesn't understand how hard it is. It's real—real tough and real hard."

"That's kinda the point of the story," Valerie said. "Life was tougher than the prodigal son thought it would be. He realized he needed his father. So he went back."

"That's what I don't buy," L said. "Once you've left, it's too hard to go back."

Valerie looked at Lincoln for a long moment. "Not if you want it bad enough," she offered. L didn't say a word. Then Valerie said, "You've been out here awhile, haven't you?" L shrugged. Valerie knew from her mission briefing that he had been missing nearly two months.

The sermon was short and about over. Valerie noticed a small Bible in the pew pocket in front of her. A bright, red ribbon stuck out of the top. It grabbed Valerie's curiosity, and she pulled the Bible out, opening it up to where the ribbon rested. It was in Acts 8. Verses 39 and 40 were highlighted.

39 When they came up out of the water, the Spirit of the Lord took Philip away; the officer never saw him again. The officer continued on his way home, full of joy.
40 But Philip appeared in a city called Azotus and preached the Good News in all the towns on the way from Azotus to Caesarea.

At first, Valerie thought they were odd verses to highlight, but her eyes opened wide when the Holy Spirit revealed the mystery to her. Valerie realized she might never know who highlighted the verses. But *this* is what had happened to her.

"I've been translated," she said aloud.

"Shhh!" L hushed. "What?"

"Like Philip in this verse here," she said pointing to the verse. "The Lord took him away from one place and the next thing Philip knew, he appeared in another. That's what happened to me."

"God does that?"

"Well, He doesn't change. It makes sense—God goes to great measures to love people. If I hadn't been under the snow, your dog might not have found me...and I might not have found you."

"Who found *who?*" Lincoln asked with a smirk. Valerie smiled back.

Reverend Bankson brought his sermon to a close. A wide smile and open arms invited his listeners to the front for an altar call. "Is there anyone who wants to come home to God today?" he asked. "Just raise your hand—I guarantee your life will change forever. Anyone?"

No one moved. He just smiled and put down his arms. Valerie wondered how many times he had done this: made an invitation and had no response. Surely he knew his listeners were not there because they wanted to be, but because they *had* to be. Most, if not all, were only there for a safe, warm night's sleep.

Valerie remembered how, on Calypso Island, so many came to hear the Word her parents preached only because they were giving away food and medical help. But Valerie's parents kept preaching. Kept giving. Kept hoping. Yes, they had hope: For if just one life was changed, it would be worth every message, every month, every year. After all, every word was a seed of hope planted in those lives.

The preacher was about to dismiss the service when suddenly a woman on the second row, dressed in common rags, stood up on her pew. Reverend Bankson was at a loss for words. All eyes went straight to her—even eyes that had been closed most of the service.

The woman shouted, "WOULD SOMEONE PLEASE TURN UP THE HEAT!"

Valerie felt embarrassed for her. Reverend Bankson nodded. "I'll check on it," he said. "Go ahead and have a seat for now."

"Oh, no you don't!" the woman shouted. "This is *my* dream and I want it warmer NOW!"

Valerie's head tilted. She recognized that voice.

The woman spun around and shouted, "Is anyone else FREEZING?!"

Valerie gasped. A few people actually raised their hands.

Valerie stood up slowly. "Uh, Missy..."

"Oh, thank God, someone I know is finally in my dream." Missy jumped down from the pew and walked back to where Valerie was, talking nonstop. "Girl, this is the most realistic dream I've ever had. I feel wide awake, but I know I can't be because obviously I would *never* be here! Check this out!"

As Missy entered the pew, she reached forward and tugged on the long, gray beard of a man sitting in front of Valerie. He yelped.

"Isn't that great?!" Missy chimed. "Now if this was real, that would be incredibly rude, not to mention embarrassing—but it's not real! Ha-ha!"

Valerie bit her lip.

"Ha-ha!" Missy repeated, a little less sure of herself.

"It's not a dream," Valerie whispered, glancing up at the bewildered preacher.

Missy's smile dropped. "But this can't be real. Just a moment ago I was at a briefing with Commander Kellie, you and the guys. Next thing I knew, I fell asleep and started having this incredible dream. I actually found myself running with a group of homeless people who led me here. Isn't that funny?! Look! My hair's a mess and I don't care!"

Missy held her blond hair straight out. It was dirty—and it *was* a mess. Valerie grabbed Missy's hand and pulled her down into the pew. Reverend Bankson moved on to other things, dismissing the group, pointing the way to a simple dinner and the sleeping area.

"Missy, this is *not* a dream," Valerie repeated. "We've been translated. God brought us from one place to another—instantly."

"But that's…"

"Exactly what happened to Philip. Remember, in Acts?" Valerie grabbed the small Bible, opened it, and shoved the high-lighted passage in Missy's face.

Missy's eyes widened.

"So this is…*real*…and I just…I…I am soooo embarrassed."

"You didn't know."

Missy jumped up and leaned over into the face of the man sitting in front of her. "I'm *so* sorry!" she apologized. "I thought this was a dream!" He rubbed his beard and grunted.

Missy sat back down and looked at her hands. "Ewwww! I'm so dirty! Gross! And I've touched a bunch of these people!"

"Missy!" Valerie scolded. A few eyes darted to the Superkid. Missy Ashton was a member of the Blue Squad, Valerie's room-mate and a good friend. She came from a high-society back-ground, which, Valerie thought, made this assignment rather ironic for her. But everyone has to grow. For now, she had exchanged her perfect, blond hair, manicured nails and fashion-able clothes for something a bit more…challenging.

"Oh! I didn't mean that like it sounded!" Missy corrected. "I just mean I'm not like"—she waved her hand at the crowd—"them."

Valerie dropped her head. Missy wasn't helping her case.

"No-no. Wait. What I mean is that… They're just not as…health-conscious. You know? I mean…"

Valerie covered her eyes. Lincoln leaned forward from behind Valerie.

"So we're sick, huh?" he asked.

Missy nodded. "Well, yeah, but only in a manner of speaking."

"You're one to talk."

Missy looked down at the rags she wore and fumbled for words.

"Missy, Lincoln Furlong," Valerie introduced. "L, Missy Ashton."

Lincoln nodded. "I'd shake your hand, but I don't want to spread my germs."

Missy's face blushed with embarrassment. Then, "Wait—is he the kid who…"

"Phase one of our mission is accomplished," Valerie stated.

✪ ✪ ✪

To Valerie's relief, Geofferson Mission's ComPhone was reactivated and she was able to contact Commander Kellie. She punched in the number and moments later her commander's face smiled at her from the small view screen. Her shoulder-length, dark-brown hair curved around her face. She wore her standard, Blue Squad uniform.

Valerie took a few moments to explain how God had translated her and Missy to the suburb of Geofferson. She also told her commander how they had found Lincoln Furlong, the young runaway they had been getting ready to search out.

"Good work, Valerie," Commander Kellie commended, her hazel eyes taking in the Superkid, "though I know it wasn't really as much your doing as the Lord's. As Proverbs 3:5-6 says, 'Trust in the Lord with all your heart and lean not on your own understanding; in all your ways acknowledge him, and he will make your paths straight.'"

Valerie smiled. "Amen. Well, with your permission, we'd like to stay for a few days and see if we can help L find his mother. He's convinced she's out on these streets somewhere."

Commander Kellie nodded. "Sounds good. The guys and I are going to start work on another project. I just received a mysterious call for help. We don't know who sent it, but they gave me an exact address where they'll be...and they told me to come alone."

Valerie twisted her lips and frowned. "That sounds a bit strange. Be careful."

"I will. Paul and Rapper and I are making plans now. They'll be backing me up."

"What about Alex?" Valerie asked.

Commander Kellie paused and stared at Valerie. "You mean he's not with you?"

Valerie shook her head. "No...should he be?"

"He disappeared the same moment you did. I just assumed when you said you guys were translated, you meant all three of you. I wonder where God sent him...?"

Valerie looked around. "Well, I'll certainly keep a lookout for him." She could see the concern in her commander's face.

"Report back to me by tomorrow if not sooner," Commander Kellie ordered. "Over and out." The screen flashed white and then went blank.

When Valerie got off the ComPhone, Missy was standing there watching her. Valerie smiled.

"I'm glad you're here with me, Val," Missy said sweetly. "You always know just when to take charge and get things under control."

Valerie shrugged. "Hey, I'm glad you're here, too. At least things are making a bit more sense now."

Both Superkids were still looking rough, but at least they had time after the sermon to throw some water on their faces and wash up a bit. Valerie was sure Missy would flip if anyone pulled out a camera, but at least they both felt cleaner, despite their rags. They also grabbed a small bite to eat.

"This is *so* not me," Missy pointed out as they walked down the mission's hallway. "I don't mean to sound harsh, but these people just live *different*."

"You feel uncomfortable here?" Valerie asked.

"To say the least," Missy responded frankly. "Check it out—they're eating soy burgers for dinner. What *is* that anyway? I just had the soup."

"You know, they're people just like you or me, Missy. The faces may be different, but the hearts are the same."

Missy didn't say anything more, but Valerie could tell she didn't quite agree. After four years as her roommate, she knew Missy pretty well.

"I'm gonna go wash my hands again," Missy said a moment later, darting into a restroom.

Valerie came to the end of the hallway. Lincoln was there, staring at the wall where the bulletin board and a painting also hung. His backpack was at his feet, resting against his tattered athletic shoes. Valerie noticed how his black hair was uneven in the back and around his ears. She wondered when he last had a haircut.

"Thinking about lending a helping hand, L?" She asked, taking note again of the fake hands dangling from the bulletin board. Lincoln snapped out of his stupor and glanced over at Valerie.

"Huh? Oh..." He looked over at the board. "No, I wasn't looking at that. I was looking at this painting."

Valerie looked at the reproduction and smiled. Though she hadn't paid it much attention earlier, she knew the painting well. She had always liked paintings, even from a young age. When she found the time to pick up a brush, she was even pretty good at working on canvas herself. Something about painting thrilled her and soothed her at the same time. The thick liquids, the brush strokes, creating a world afresh...

"This is one of my favorites," Valerie noted. "It's a Rembrandt."

"What does that mean?"

Valerie chuckled. "That's the name of the man who painted it. He painted this one sometime between 1660 and his death in 1669."

Lincoln touched the smooth print. "It's old. But I like it," he admitted.

Valerie leaned in. "This one's called *The Return of the Prodigal Son.* It's based on the Bible story Reverend Bankson was preaching about earlier. Kind of fitting, huh?"

Valerie took in the portrait. There was the father on the left-hand side, a tall, gentle man, leaning down and placing his hands on his son's back. The son—the prodigal son—had just returned to his father. He was kneeling before him, his head on his father's chest, his feet sticking out behind him, one shoe so worn it was hanging off his bare foot. The son was in drab, shabby apparel, the father in brilliant red.

Then, on the right-hand side, two men watched. Valerie often wondered what they were thinking. Were they being critical? Were they touched? Or did they even understand? And on the left, in the back, was a woman. Was this the boy's mother? What was *she* thinking? What kind of emotion was bursting from her heart?

But to Valerie, the most mysterious character of all was the one in the center of the painting. He was almost unnoticeable...he almost blended into the background. Was this the older brother in the story of the prodigal son? Was this the one who couldn't understand why his father would take his long-lost brother back? Was this the one who could have partaken of his father's inheritance at any time, but never asked?

Lincoln moved his hand over to the prodigal son's bare foot. He rolled his finger down the dirty sole.

"You really think the father would accept his son back like this?"

"If he's a loving father, yes," Valerie reassured him.

Lincoln looked at the painting for several more moments. "I'm a long way from home," he whispered.

Valerie cocked her head. "It's just across town," she said.

L took his finger away from the print. "I wish."

Valerie touched his arm again and promised that she and Missy would help him find his mother. L jerked his arm away and made his way to the cafeteria.

As Missy rejoined Valerie, she nodded her head toward L. "What's got him miffed?" she asked.

Valerie let out a long breath. "He just wants to go home," she replied.

Missy roared, holding her stomach and pointing. "Ha! What in the world is *that?!*"

Lincoln didn't find anything humorous about his dog, Snicker. He retrieved him from the side room and stuffed him into his backpack once more.

"This is Snicker," he replied defensively. "I found him one day. He and I found a silver pen at the same time. Hey— you don't see him laughing at you!"

"I may look bad," Missy admitted, "but that dog has one up on me! Ha!"

Snicker wagged his tail.

Valerie rubbed the back of her tightened neck. The three adventurers had slept well, but not comfortably. The mattresses were old and bumpy, giving Valerie the sensation of sleeping on an elephant's back. Not that she'd ever slept on an elephant's back before, but if she ever did, she imagined it would have felt just like her night at Geofferson Mission.

Breakfast in the crammed cafeteria consisted of powdered, scrambled eggs and watered-down orange juice. Missy had only taken three bites when a man passed behind her and sneezed.

From that point on, she could see imaginary germs waltzing on the eggs. "Grosses me out," she muttered.

Despite the circumstances and the constant feeling that she didn't have things under control, Valerie found herself thankful. At least they had a place to stay. How had the Apostle Paul put it in Philippians 4:12? "I have learned the secret of being content in any and every situation." Valerie placed her hand over her heart. To be content in any and every situation: That was what she wanted.

She also found herself praying for Reverend Bankson. The middle-aged man had opened the shelter, preached to the lost, stayed up all night, then cooked breakfast and served it himself. *What dedication,* Valerie thought. He even did it without receiving any thanks—or ever asking for any.

But Geofferson Mission was about to be behind them. Now, red-eyed and messy-haired, the team of Valerie, Missy, Lincoln and Snicker was ready to embark on its quest.

As they headed for the exit, Valerie wondered aloud, "How come everybody's leaving? You'd think they'd rather stay in here where it's warm."

"They have to leave," L said. "The mission closes after breakfast."

Valerie felt her heart drop, despite the fact that she knew the mission was a one-man operation. "But it's cold outside!"

"Well, it makes sense, I guess," Missy interjected. "By making them leave for the day, maybe some of them will realize they have to do a little work for a living."

"Oh, please," L shot back at Missy. "Don't tell me you really think these people are all on the street because they're just lazy."

"Well, no, I…"

L continued, "Some couldn't find work. And some can't work. And some..." L looked down, thoughtfully. "Some have just lost hope."

"Well, *I'd* never be on the street," Missy said matter-of-factly.

"You *are* on the street," L pressed, turning his coal-colored eyes on her.

"Enough, you two," Valerie said. "And, Missy, don't forget you're a Superkid. We need to be a reflection of that, remember?"

"And who put you in charge?" L challenged.

Valerie stopped in her tracks just outside the mission. "Do you really want to find your mom?" she asked.

L squinted. "What kind of question is that? Of course I do."

"You said yourself that you could use our help. Now, I haven't been out here on the streets long, but I can tell it's no fun. L, I want to help." Valerie grabbed Missy's arm. *"We* want to help."

L looked at Missy. "I *do* want to help," Missy agreed.

"I'm not trying to rule over you," Valerie said softly to L. "I just want to keep things under control so we can find your mother."

"OK," Lincoln said, pulling his dirty jacket tightly around his chest. He rolled his shoulders, repositioning his backpack. "What should we do first?"

"First we need to pray," Valerie instructed. "Without God, there's not much we can do."

Valerie grabbed Missy's hand and the two girls reached for L's. He pulled his hands away and kicked the snow.

"No!" L shouted. He whirled around and Snicker, still in his backpack, whimpered. His wet, button nose was peeking out of an opening in the top. "I'm not going to pray!" L proclaimed. "God doesn't listen anyway!"

Missy leaned over to Valerie. "I think he's got some pent-up anger issues."

"Where did that come from?" Valerie asked Lincoln. "And how can you say that? Psalm 4:3 says that the Lord always hears when we call to Him. Psalm 37:39 says He's our stronghold in times of trouble."

L hastily removed his backpack and set it down. When it hit the ground, the top popped open and Snicker jumped out.

L mumbled something about how much Valerie quoted Scripture. Then he waved his hand in the air and shouted, "You know, that's a perfect fairy tale, but the reality is that He's either not listening or He just plain doesn't care!"

Missy opened her mouth to say something, but L continued, "You wanna know how I can say that? I'll tell you! Less than a year ago, I had a dad. A good dad—a great dad. But one day, I came home and he was dead. And I prayed God would bring him back to life. I prayed that he had just fainted or just lost consciousness...but no. He…" L took a long breath. "Then my mom said we had to move because she couldn't afford it. I prayed again. 'God, help us to stay here. God, help us.' But we moved. And the next thing I knew, she was gone too! God let my dad and my mom be taken away! He's God, isn't He?! Why didn't He do something?!"

Lincoln stared at Valerie and Missy. The two girls stared back. Neither could find the words.

"You...you can't stop praying," Valerie offered.

"Why not?" L asked. He pointed to the sky, bold with his words. "He stopped listening."

Lincoln wasn't much in the mood for talking, Valerie could tell. Since their last conversation, he had made it a point to walk at least two paces behind the girls. The only time he spoke was when Snicker started to stray. For Valerie, L's attitude was making adjusting to the streets more stressful.

She understood why he felt the way he did, but that didn't change God's Word. *What it says,* she thought to herself, *is the* Truth—*no matter what the circumstances say...no matter how bad Satan makes things...no matter how hard they are to digest.*

Valerie also knew that now wasn't the time for L to turn his back on God. Right now was when he needed God's guidance and the comfort of the Holy Spirit the most. But Valerie realized that as long as L refused to listen, she was just preaching to herself. *Father God, bring Lincoln to a point where he sees how lost he is without You,* she silently prayed.

The wintry air felt like invisible ice, rolling over Valerie's face and threatening to seep into any opening in her clothing. The sun was finally out, but there wasn't any warmth coming from it. Valerie was a bit surprised at how gray everything looked amid the testy weather. Leafless trees, crunching snow, slick ice, frosted windows—nothing seemed to have so much as an inkling of life. The streets were empty, save an occasional, homeless wanderer who was just as empty of vitality as the old, crumbling buildings.

Some of the wanderers were tall, some were short, some were young, some were old, most were slow. This was the part of the city left for them, the outcasts of society, who had nowhere else to go. As Valerie, Missy, Lincoln and Snicker rounded a corner, Valerie gasped as she saw dozens of homeless men and women standing in an open lot. Like a small army, they stood around fires crackling in trash cans, keeping warm. Several talked and all faced the fires, soaking themselves with the emanating warmth.

"This is where we'll start," Valerie said. "Besides, I could use some of that warmth." She moved toward a trash can that had some room for her and her crew. They walked up, crunching snow beneath their tattered shoes. An old woman in gray and purple slid aside to allow them all entrance. Valerie said, "Thank you," and the woman smiled sweetly at her, toothless.

The heat was welcoming, even though it smelled a little like burning paint. Snicker, with his own coat of fur, seemed content. Valerie watched the steam of her breath explode into the air and then vanish.

"It's a cold, cold day," the old woman in gray and purple said to the group.

"Too cold," a young man on the other side of the trash can agreed. "I remember a day like this when I was in Iceland."

"You mean Iceland, the country?" Missy asked, curious.

The man nodded politely. He had cleanshaven, reddish skin and messy hair. "You name it, I've been there."

"France?" Missy challenged.

"I backpacked across it."

"Tibet?" Missy quizzed.

"Climbed the Himalayas—even Everest."

Valerie questioned, "All the way to the top?"

"I wish," the man said. Valerie smiled politely. At more than 29,000 feet, Mount Everest was the world's highest peak—and only a few people had ever made it to the top.

Missy twisted her lip. "So if you're so adventurous, what are you doing on the streets?"

The man's bottom lip protruded slightly. After a moment, he reached down and pulled off the brown glove over his right hand.

"I got the shakes two years ago."

"The shakes?" Valerie asked.

The man held his hand out flat before him and it trembled like it was freezing.

"Not many places will hire you when you can't even hold a pencil to fill out the application," the man noted.

Missy began, "But there's…"

"I've tried," the man interrupted, bitterly. "No one's hiring a man with the shakes. And I spent all my money on doctors who couldn't cure me."

The man reached into his pocket and pulled out a flask. Valerie heard the liquor slosh inside as the flask shook in his hand. He raised it to his mouth and took a drink. Then he clumsily reclosed the bottle. Before he returned it to his pocket, he held it out and toasted Missy.

"This is the only doctor who'll help me now," he said, grimly. Missy was speechless.

Valerie spoke up. "That's not true," she said. "Jesus can cure you of the shakes and the bottle. Just ask…"

Before Valerie could finish her sentence, the man turned around and walked away. He completely ignored her—as if she hadn't even been speaking to him.

"That's so sad," Missy whispered, pulling at her hands.

"That's nothing," the old woman in purple and gray corrected. Then she was off, too.

Several minutes of humbling silence passed. Valerie looked at Missy. Missy looked at Valerie. Lincoln raised his eyebrows as if to say, "That's life." Finally Valerie said to Missy and L, "C'mon. We've got to get to work."

"What are we going to do?" Missy wondered, pushing away

her somber thoughts.

"Well," Valerie began, "L's pretty sure his mom has been living on the streets for the past couple of months. If she has, someone around here is sure to have seen her. Let's start asking."

"I've asked all these people," L spoke up.

Valerie let out a long breath. "Then we'll ask them again. Let's split up. *Someone* must have seen her."

✪   ✪   ✪

"Never heard of her."

"Who?"

"She could be anywhere."

"Nobody like that around here."

"Nope, never."

Valerie found it hard to believe that not one person had seen or heard of Elly Furlong. But what she found harder to believe was how many responded with a single, hopeless, haunting phrase: "Bet the raiders got her."

Finally, Valerie decided to ask. A dark-skinned man, presumably in his 30s, was surprised she hadn't heard of the raiders.

"The raiders," he said pointedly. "They come out here to get lab rats."

"Who are they?" Valerie asked. The man shook his head.

"Can't say. Never seen 'em in the light. They only come out at night. Like dogcatchers, they are. They sneak around. We hear 'em and we sound a silent alarm—whispers. We whisper to each other, 'Run! Run!' and anybody who has half a brain takes off in any which direction they can. 'Cause I tell you, no one who ever goes with the raiders comes back. But we know they're used as lab rats."

"But if no one has ever come back, how do you know?"

Valerie wondered. "Maybe they're taking them away to help them. Maybe they're…"

"No," the homeless man responded. "People who bind you to take you, they don't help you. They come for the weakest of us, and when they find them, they get them. You stay and watch and you'll see. It ain't no pleasant sight."

Valerie nodded and thanked the man. He smiled weakly and turned away, once again preoccupied with a fire in a barrel.

Valerie made a mental note to ask L about the raiders and their raids on the homeless. He had mentioned them briefly when they first met. What if his mother *had* been captured? In that case, they'd just have to pay the raiders a visit.

Valerie looked around the area to see if there was anyone the group hadn't asked. Her eyes surveyed the crowd…and suddenly she realized Missy was nowhere in sight.

"Missy?" she called out. A few people turned their heads. Valerie quickly walked over to Lincoln.

"L, have you seen Missy?"

L nodded. She could tell he had cooled down. "Yeah. She went into that corner diner. She said she'd be out in a minute."

Valerie hadn't even noticed the diner there earlier. It was as drab as the surrounding buildings and almost looked vacant. But there were a couple of dented hovercars parked at the curb, indicating some sort of life inside. Something about it gave Valerie a "check" in her spirit; something wasn't right. Valerie decided to peek in on her friend. "C'mon," she said to L. He and Snicker tagged along without protest.

"You'd think the diner would be packed with people," Valerie noted. "It has to be warmer in there than out here at the barrels."

"The people inside probably hate the homeless," L responded matter-of-factly. "Most of the businesses that are still open around here do. 'Course, if you ask me, they should just get out of here if they don't like it."

There was no traffic, so crossing the street was no chore, and moments later Valerie was pulling on the old door handle.

The door creaked open and warm air blasted Valerie in the face. It felt good, but the air was thick with smoke, burning Valerie's eyes. A couple of regulars sat quietly at a booth, sipping on alcoholic beverages and watching a hanging television set. The TV was louder than necessary, spouting off some biased chatter about a "great new form of justice in development by NME. Criminals will actually be jailed in another world!" *That figures,* Valerie thought. *Rather than helping criminals, they want to send them to another planet.* NME stood for Notoriously Malicious Enterprises—the organization dedicated to corrupting the world while selling lies as truth. They had long been rivals of Superkid Academy, and Valerie didn't put much stock in what they had to say.

Behind a counter, the owner of the diner wasn't enticed with the broadcast either. He was too busy dealing with a customer— one Valerie was happy to see: Missy. Valerie and Lincoln stepped inside. Snicker waited on the sidewalk.

"No, I don't have any money on me," Missy was saying, "but my dad is Gregg Ashton, owner of Ashton Clothiers in Nautical. He can debit…"

"Right," the owner snapped back in a thick, sharp accent. "Now get outta here before I call the authorities."

"Give me a break," Missy pleaded. "I'm just asking for a little something to munch on. You have my word—I'll pay you."

The owner of the corner diner leaned over the counter, into Missy's face. "If I feed you, I gotta feed all your deadbeat friends, too. And giving away food ain't no way to run an eatery. Now get *out* or I'm calling the cops."

Missy backed up in shock. Valerie bit her lip. Missy had turned people off at times with her upfront attitude, but never with her looks. This was definitely a first.

Lincoln stepped forward and, to Valerie's surprise, grabbed Missy's arm. "C'mon, Missy, let's go. You don't want food from here, anyway."

Missy turned to L. "No—this isn't right. I haven't done anything wrong. I'm staying until…"

Screeeeeech!

The two regulars lost interest in the television broadcast. They had pushed their chairs back and were now standing. Before Valerie or the others knew what was happening, all three men were coming at them.

Missy was the first grabbed by the collar of her jacket, L next and Valerie third. "Hey!" Valerie cried in protest. Missy added, "You can't do this!"

"Watch them," L said subtly, the voice of experience.

Smack!

The front door shot open, the cold air hit their faces once again and the trio went flying—right over Snicker, who barked at the bullies.

Bam! Bam! Bam!

All three hit the snow-packed ground like snowplows, clearing tiny paths in the walkway. They heard laughter as the diner door closed with a reverberating clank.

Then Missy screamed. Valerie, on her belly, looked over and

saw two big, fluffy boots in front of Missy's face. Missy scrambled to get up, pushing aside the thick snow. She looked up to see the face of a homeless man, smiling. He was a large man, with thinning, wispy, white hair and a beard like Old Saint Nick. He wore a brown patchwork suit with wide lapels and a vest. He reached down with a rough hand to help Missy up. She accepted his offer.

"Thank you," she said.

The homeless man turned momentarily and coughed a horrible cough and then turned back to Missy. "I've missed you, Nadine," he said in a deep and simple voice. "But I finally found you."

Missy squinted. "My name's not Nadine, it's Missy," she explained. The man's face crinkled as he smiled.

"You can't fool me," he said, touching her nose with his finger. "I've known you all my life, Nadine." He giggled.

Missy raised her head to the sky. "Why me?" she asked.

Lincoln, already up, helped Valerie get on her feet again. Snicker, the poodle/cocker spaniel/Chihuahua, observed everyone with excitement, wagging his tail.

"Missy, next time you feel like wandering, ask me first," L said. "I've already tried going in every open place around here and no one seems to care how cold it is. Especially these guys."

Missy brushed herself off. "I'll remember that," she said.

Valerie stomped the ground, knocking the frigid, packed snow off her pants. "We didn't even do anything wrong," she protested. Valerie slapped the wall of the building, trying to make a statement to those inside, but just hurting her hand.

"Valerie seems a bit upset," L said to Missy.

"She gets like that sometimes when things aren't going the way they should be," Missy responded.

Lincoln said sarcastically, "News flash—what around here *is* the way it should be?"

"What is this?" Valerie shouted, shaking her hands in front of her. "A commentary?"

Missy smiled widely.

"Well, it *isn't* right," Valerie whispered.

"If it's any consolation, I agree with you," Missy said. She shook her head, tossing any snow remnants from her blond hair.

The homeless man tried putting his hand on Missy's shoulder, but she slipped past him. "Hey, what do you say we get on the move, here? The sooner we find Elly, the sooner we can all go home."

Suddenly the homeless man's eyes grew wide. "Ohhh, I know Elly! Elly is a nice friend."

Lincoln's attention was captured. "You know Elly? How do you know Elly?"

"Elly's a friend I visit. I visit lots of friends."

"Elly's my mom. Where is she?"

"Elly is a nice friend," he repeated in his deep, boyish voice.

Valerie intervened. "What's your name?" she asked the man.

"My name is Ralph," he responded simply, holding out his hand. "Ralph Ruther. What's your name?"

"I'm Valerie," Valerie said politely, shaking his hand. "And this is Missy, and this is Lincoln and this is Snicker." The dog barked. Ralph laughed.

"Pleased to meet you," he said sweetly.

"Do you know where Elly is?" Valerie asked.

Ralph nodded. "Yes, I know where Elly is. I will take you to her if Nadine is going, too." He looked at Missy.

"Oh—no," Missy protested. "I am *not* doing this."

Lincoln stepped forward and patted her on the back. "Of course Nadine is going," he said to Ralph, smiling. "Lead the way."

What should have been a 20-minute walk brought them into late afternoon, after Ralph took three wrong turns and forgot twice what they were doing. Valerie found Ralph's demeanor kind and pleasant, and she was hoping Missy thought the same. She could tell Missy was gritting her teeth every time Ralph called her Nadine. But she was a good sport.

L appeared quiet, but excited. Valerie could only imagine what was going through his mind. He would finally find his mother—and he probably had a hundred questions for her. *Why did you leave? What happened? Where have you been living? Why didn't you try to contact me? Why didn't you tell me you were leaving? Did you think about me often? Did you want me to find you?* Valerie wanted to know the answers to those questions herself.

This final alley Ralph led them down was dark and dirty. The snow was black, peppered with deteriorating paper cups and fast-food restaurant wrappers. Rusty fire escapes climbed the alley walls like metal snakes.

Partway down the alley, Ralph stopped in his tracks. He pointed forward.

"Elly lives around that corner," he said plainly.

"You're not going?" Valerie wondered.

Ralph shook his head. "I'd better stay here."

"Good idea," L said to Ralph. "If there's a raid, someone

has to warn us. The back of an alley's not the place you want to be caught."

Ralph nodded. Valerie noticed the worry lines in his forehead.

"I really want to know who these raiders are," Valerie said.

"No, you really don't," L offered.

"Missy, why don't you stay and keep Ralph company." Valerie suggested. Missy nearly protested, but when Ralph gave her a big smile, she gave in.

Valerie and Lincoln trudged on. Snicker accompanied them, sniffing the ground for clues.

As they approached, Valerie's heartbeat quickened. She began to notice things she hadn't noticed before—the hollow sounds of their footsteps in the alley, the whisper of wind in the air, the stench of decaying trash on the ground. This was no place for someone to live.

When they rounded the corner, Valerie's stomach leapt in anticipation. A large box was wedged there, on its side. A stick held the door—a flap on the box—open. Inside, a soiled sheet was crumpled into a crude, makeshift floor. Valerie closed her eyes as a lump formed in her throat.

Lincoln voiced her thoughts: "How could anyone live here? She could have at least come to the mission."

"I don't know," Valerie whispered, feeling tears well up in her eyes. "I don't know what could drive a person to this."

"Well, I do," Lincoln said sadly.

Snicker walked over to the sheet inside the box, pushed it around and lay down.

"Just look at this place," Lincoln said softly. He looked around a bit, but didn't find anything that reminded him of his mother. He leaned against a hard wall and slid to the ground.

Valerie sat down across from him, wondering what to do next. From his backpack, L pulled out a photo and handed it to Valerie. The picture was a studio shot of Lincoln, his mother and his father. All three were smiling widely, sitting close together.

L looked like his father, Valerie thought. All three Furlongs had beautiful olive skin and straight, black hair. L's cheekbones, smile and nose were more like his father's...but he had his mother's coal-colored eyes.

"It used to be in a frame, but I traded the frame for food," L explained, reaching out for the photo. Valerie handed it back, letting out a long breath. Lincoln ran his right hand along the photo's side, carefully, lovingly.

"He had a heart attack," L said without emotion. "It happened just before I got home from school." Lincoln pressed a palm against his right eye. "I should have been there," he confessed. "I was on my way home from school and I...I went into a comic book store to look around. When I finally got home, I found him on the floor, facedown. I called the medics." L sniffed. His chin quivered. "They said if we had found him sooner, they might have been able to save him...but it was too late."

Valerie shook her head. "Lincoln, you didn't know. There was nothing you could have done."

"There *was* something I could have done!" L protested. Then he quieted down again. "I could have saved his life. If I hadn't gone to the comic book store, I... Why didn't God tell me, Valerie? You say you're a Superkid—tell me! Why did He let me go to the comic book store? He could have saved my dad."

"Lincoln," Valerie soothed, "this is not your fault and it's not God's fault. Satan came in and took advantage of you. Don't let that happen again by turning your back on God."

"You've never lost anyone, have you?" L challenged. Valerie didn't answer. She couldn't. No, she hadn't lost anyone. Ever. Her mother almost died once from a fatal disease on Calypso Island, but God miraculously healed her when Valerie prayed. That was the closest she had ever come to a death in her family. She realized she couldn't really fathom what L was feeling. Not *really.*

"I know you have a lot of questions," Valerie said, "but the only answer I know is Jesus. He's your hope, L. Turning your back on Him is the worst thing you could do right now. Your dad knew Jesus, right?"

"Yeah, so?"

"So your dad is in heaven now. He wants to see you one day. Until then, you have to keep your hope alive."

Lincoln sneered. Valerie got up, walked over and sat down beside L. She placed her hand on his arm. "Lincoln," she said, "you have a heavenly Father who loves you more than you know. He's waiting with open arms for you to come back. You remember that picture in the mission, the one of the prodigal son? Do you remember how the father held his son? Every day he had been looking for him to return. Finally one day he did...and the father received him as though he had never left. God wants you to come back to Him, L. But you have to take the first step back. Let Him help you find your mother."

L opened his mouth to say something when suddenly Snicker's head raised and his ears popped up. Valerie looked at L.

"What's wrong?" she asked.

L listened to the air, then shook his head. "I don't know…"

"GET OUT!!!" An old woman came in, swinging an old

umbrella. Her gray hair was in a bun and her pale face was full of wrinkles. She looked frail in her long coat, despite the fact that she was swinging like Babe Ruth. Missy and Ralph were close behind, but trying to keep a safe distance.

"THIS IS MY HOME!" she cried. "GET OUT!!"

"Your home?" Valerie asked, curiously. Missy was in the background, shrugging her shoulders.

"YES! I claimed it from the last!" she shouted.

"The *last?"* Valerie repeated after her. "You mean Elly Furlong?"

The woman stopped swinging for a moment. "You know Elly?" She leaned in, frowning. "What do you want with Elly?"

"I'm her son," L explained. "I've been looking for her."

The woman squinted at L dubiously. She grabbed his chin. "You do kinda look like her," she admitted. Then she peered closer. "She spoke of you often."

"She did?"

The woman nodded. "You're the reason she went back when she couldn't make things work." The woman raised the umbrella. "Gave me her spot." She pointed the umbrella at Valerie. "It's mine." Valerie put her hands in the air.

"She went back?" L inquired. "Back where? And when?"

The woman chewed on her cheek and then answered, "About 10 days ago, it was. Said something about an apartment."

Lincoln was already running out of the alley. Valerie scooted around, keeping good distance from the umbrella tip. "Thank you!" she shouted, escaping. Snicker barked and trailed after her, running under the woman's legs. Missy was close behind, pulling Ralph.

The woman kept shaking her umbrella at them until they could see her no longer.

As they ran, L turned to Valerie. "I've been looking for her all this time," he said with a huff, "and she returned to the apartment! I knew she would!"

Valerie hoped he was right.

"This is home?" Valerie asked, observing the cracked walls and worn floor.

"No, it's not," Lincoln replied. "This is just a temporary place to live. Until we get back on our feet."

As they reached Lincoln's apartment, a door creaked open across the hall and a deep-set eye peeked out.

"Just ignore him," L whispered, angling his head back toward the observer. "That's the landlord and he's a little strange—comes after intruders with a shotgun. Creeps me out. But as long as we act like we know what we're doing, he'll probably just ignore us."

"Probably?" Missy asked rhetorically. L smiled.

The door across the hall shut with a bang. Snicker jumped.

Valerie's stomach felt like it was full of butterflies again. The excitement of mother and son reuniting was thrilling— and it would finally happen this time. Mission accomplished!

L knocked and waited. He straightened his shirt. No one answered.

Ralph looked at Missy and smiled, his white mustache lifting with his rosy cheekbones. Missy smiled back.

Lincoln fumbled with the doorknob. The door across the way opened again and the eye peered out. L held the knob tight, then slammed against the door with his shoulder. Valerie heard a *pop!* and the door to the Furlongs' apartment opened.

Missy asked, "Is it always so easy to break in?"

"We were never too concerned about burglars," L replied. "They're not much of a problem when you don't have anything to steal."

Without hesitation, the crew shuffled in and closed the door behind them, happy to be away from the guy across the hall.

As they entered, Valerie heard L gasp.

"This isn't our furniture," he said. Then he turned to Valerie. "Do you think she got new furniture?"

"This doesn't look so new," Missy observed.

"Mom?" L shouted. No one answered.

"I'm sorry, L," Valerie said. "But if someone else has moved in, we have to go."

Ralph smiled and put an arm around Missy. His white beard bounced as he said, "It's just like our home, isn't it, Nadine?"

Missy closed her eyes. "I'm not Nadine," she stated flatly.

Lincoln walked through the room. "I don't understand," he said. "Where's our stuff?"

"Maybe someone *did* rob you," Missy suggested.

"And then replaced it with different furniture, locking the door on the way out? I don't think so," L reasoned.

L pointed to the brown sofa in the living room. "That's where our sofa was, too...but it looked better there than that one does," he noted. "Our coffee table was there...and this is where the kitchen table was. You don't think..."

"What?" Valerie wondered.

"You don't think she moved without me, do you?" L completed his thought. Again, Valerie felt at a loss for words. She didn't quite know how to answer. No, she didn't know for sure. It was unsettling.

Valerie was about to answer L when a deep growl rolled

from Snicker's throat.

Rrrrrrrrrrrrrr...

"What is it?" Missy asked.

"What is it, boy?" Lincoln wondered, kneeling down to his dog. The mutt's ears flipped up and his brown eyes locked on the front door.

Rrrrrrrrrrrrrr...

"Snicker?"

The dog's bark came only a split second before the front door blew open with a crash. All four adventurers screamed from surprise, leaping back.

Standing in the doorway, breathing deeply, was a man with oily, black hair and a shotgun. Valerie recognized his deep-set eye as the one that had peered out from across the hall.

Lincoln stood in front of the girls and Ralph, his arms stretched out in limited protection. "Don't shoot!" L shouted. "This is my apartment!"

The man grunted and cocked the shotgun. "You homeless scum lier. I'm the landlord and I don't know you. You're just trying to break in and steal something to eat!"

"This really *is* my apartment!" L tried to reason with the maniac. "Or—at least it *was!* I'm Lincoln Furlong. I lived here about three months ago."

"I don't remember the name 'Furlong,'" the man argued. "Besides, I threw the last people's stuff outta here weeks ago— they came up missing."

"We're not missing!" L cried. "I'm telling you—it's my apartment!"

"You got proof?!" the man shouted, the curls on his forehead jarring as he stepped forward. "No! You don't!"

BAM!

A gunshot tore through the air, blowing through the wall. Missy screamed and Valerie stood in shock. Ralph ran into the larger of two bedrooms behind them.

Missy whirled around and followed Ralph. Snicker took refuge behind Lincoln's legs. Valerie grabbed L by the collar and pulled him into the bedroom with the others. Snicker willingly followed. Valerie was hoping there would be a way out— a fire escape, a window, anything. There was nothing.

"We've got to get out of here! This guy is nuts!" Missy shouted.

"No kidding!" L agreed.

The man entered the doorway and cocked his shotgun again. Valerie gulped. Snicker growled. Then it happened.

Beneath his long sleeve, the man's silver bracelet slid out, dangling in the air. It caught Snicker's eye. The dog, overcome with excitement, wagged its tail and charged forward. The man's eyes grew big as Snicker leapt in the air, straight for the bracelet, and snapped down on the man's wrist.

BAM!

The gun went off again, this time shooting right between Valerie's feet. But she didn't have time to stand in shock. The man shouted out in pain and the group took advantage of the distraction. Together, they rammed forward and barreled by the man, knocking him off his feet.

Snicker had the man's bracelet in his mouth, but suddenly realized he had to decide whether he was going to keep the bracelet or join his friends. With a bark and another wag of his tail, he let go, trotted over the man's face and joined his friends.

The group darted out of the apartment and into the hall,

running for the elevator. When they reached it, L pushed the button and they waited.

And they waited.

And they heard a grunt come from L's apartment.

And they waited.

Another grunt.

The doors slid open and L hopped inside. He just about hit the "L" button, to send the elevator down to the lobby, when Valerie had an idea.

"Does this place have a fire escape?" she asked L. He affirmed her suspicion with a nod.

"Everyone get in the stairwell!" she ordered in a hush. The group obeyed without question. Valerie waited in the hall.

And waited.

And heard footsteps coming.

Closer...

Closer...

Valerie hit the "B" basement button and then the door "CLOSE" button. She exited the elevator and ran to the stairwell. Just as the man ran into the hallway, he saw the elevator doors closing. He ran forward at full speed and slid between the closing doors at the last second. The doors completely shut.

Valerie smiled. "Yes! He's heading to the basement. Meanwhile, we have some time. Let's get out of here!"

"But he'll expect us to go straight down!" L said.

"That's why we're going to the roof," Valerie pointed out. "After awhile, we'll take the fire escape down and out."

Lincoln smiled. "Not a bad plan," he said. "You've had experience at this, haven't you?"

❖ ❖ ❖

Valerie, Lincoln, Missy, Ralph and Snicker exploded onto the apartment building roof, nearly giddy from their close call.

"Did you see the look on his face when Snicker was coming at him?!" Lincoln shouted, laughing.

Missy reached down and roughed up the dog's head. "Didn't think you had it in you," she complimented. Snicker wagged his tail.

"It's cold up here," Ralph noted. Valerie agreed. "We'll go down in a few minutes," she promised, "after we've given that guy some time to give up on finding us."

Within moments, as they waited, the four took choice seats on half walls at the edge of the roof. They sat quietly, catching their breath, gazing into the evening sky. Valerie could see miles upon miles of city lights, glimmering in the darkness. Nighttime came earlier in the winter, a phenomenon not as easily seen on her home island of Calypso. There, almost every night of the year, Valerie could lie in bed and the sky would be the same: deep purplish-blue, speckled with twinkling stars.

The sky was different in the city, on the mainland. In some ways it was lighter because of the shine of city lights, and not as easily defined. In other ways it was darker, because not as many stars were visible. Between the air pollution and the glare of streetlights, they were simply washed out to the human eye.

But the moon was the same. It glared down, its reflection reminding each of them that the sun was just around the corner, ready to pop back up in a matter of hours. Then warmth and light would return...and hope. It was the first breath of fresh air Valerie had enjoyed since this whirlwind of a mission started.

Valerie was a bit surprised when L, looking at the stars,

spoke up and said, "Do you really think God is watching us right now, really caring about each one of us?"

Valerie smiled, star-gazing. "I have no doubt."

"Yeah," L continued, "but I mean, He made all this—the stars, the moon, the world.... Do you really think He cares about what I'm thinking right now? About what I'm feeling? About where my mom is? I mean, compared to all that"—L waved at the sky—"I'm pretty small."

"The Bible says in 1 Corinthians 1:27 that God chose the foolish things of the world to confound the wise. Lincoln, it's beyond my comprehension, too. But Psalm 139:17-18 says His thoughts toward you outnumber all the grains of sand in the seas. He's thinking about you all the time. He's your Father, L. He cares about you. He loves you."

Lincoln nodded. "You sure do know a lot of Scripture," he said.

Valerie giggled. "And I'm still trying to whip Alex in a Superkid Manual Memory Marathon." She explained that Alex was a friend of hers at Superkid Academy.

Suddenly Snicker raised his head and his ears popped up.

Missy put her hand on her head. "Oh, I hate it when he does that," she complained. "What is it this time?"

Ralph stood up. He tapped Missy on the shoulder. She stood with him. Valerie and L stood, too.

"Nadine, listen," Ralph said to Missy. Valerie heard it, too. The sound was intermittent and far away, but it was distinct. It sounded like ocean waves hitting a shoreline. It sounded like it was saying, *Run... Run...*

The group looked over the side of the building. From 10 stories up, the people looked like toy soldiers, but Valerie could see them. They were dashing through the shadows like spies... except they were running in terror. Fleeing.

"It's a raid," Ralph said sadly.

"What's that sound?" Missy wondered.

"It's the homeless warning others of the raid," L explained. "They're whispering. It's the signal to run and hide."

"We've got to do something!" Valerie insisted.

Lincoln shook his head. "There's nothing we can do but wait until it's over."

Valerie remembered how the man in the park told her they came like dogcatchers. And he was right. Slowly, like a cat on the prowl, a silent, air-powered truck hovered down the street. It lurked through shadows, hunting for prey to devour.

As it sailed down the road, once in a while a person in hiding would get scared and dart out, hoping to escape a close call. Some would scream, others would just run, run, run.... People treated like dogs....

"No...*NOOOO!*" L shouted, startling them all. He ran down the edge of the rooftop, trying to get a better look. Valerie was on his heels.

"What?" she asked.

"There!" he pointed down to the street at a lone person running under the streetlights. "That's my mom! I'm sure of it!"

Lincoln ran to the nearest fire escape, on the south side of the building. He swung over onto it with a bang. Below, the black hovertruck was closing in on his mother. Valerie watched as he bounded down the fire escape, taking steps three at a time. He himself had said there was nothing they could do to help, but that was before his mother was involved. Valerie knew L would give it all he had.

L was three stories down already, but the flying vehicle was still gaining. From above, the hovertruck looked like a dark square floating in his mother's direction. Then all at once, it stopped. The back popped open and a soldier, dressed in a black uniform, hopped out. He took off after L's mom.

L continued down, three steps or more at a time, his heavy footsteps echoing in the night. *Wham!*

L hit a stair, slick from the snow and ice—and went down the stairs like he was a bowling ball. His left foot shot out behind him and squeezed into the open space between two stairs. L struggled to get up, anxiously twisting his leg like rubber. In a desperate attempt, he tore his shoe loose, ripping off the sole in the process. L didn't care. He continued as fast as he could. He made it halfway down, but he still wasn't close enough. As the man below gained on his mother, L cried out to her.

"Mom!!!"

Elly Furlong, recognizing her son's voice, hesitated in her

run. For a moment, Lincoln looked hopeful...and Valerie was sure his mother did, too. But the hesitation was all the uniformed soldier needed. With exact precision he pointed a handheld remote at her and pushed a button. The soldier stopped running as a stream of green, electric light shot forward out of the unit and hit Elly in the small of her back. Then it expanded, surrounding her. The green light turned into a grid pattern, forming a free-standing, instant cage.

Elly smacked into the side of the cage and an electric surge rippled through her being. She cried out in surprise and pain and fell to the ground, losing consciousness. L cried out again, but didn't receive so much as a glance from the soldier.

The green, electric grid powered off and the soldier grabbed Elly, electronically handcuffing her in a pair of thick metal cuffs. The hovertruck pulled up and she was placed inside a back hatch. The soldier locked the back, then entered the craft and, like a whip, it shot off at full speed.

L was left standing halfway down the fire escape, speechless.

✪ ✪ ✪

Ralph watched, pulling on his white beard.

"The raiders come and get the weakest ones," he said after a long pause, as L climbed back up the fire escape. Ralph reached over and placed a kind arm around Missy. "I'm glad you got away, Nadine. I thought you were lost forever."

Valerie noticed Missy's face suddenly flood with understanding.

"Nadine was taken by the raiders?" she asked.

Ralph nodded. "But you made it back," he said, then he coughed. "They didn't hurt you."

Missy looked at the ground and then slowly put her own arm

around Ralph's back. "Yeah," she said softly.

Valerie closed her eyes. It was just one more thing that wasn't right...one more thing that had gone awry.

As Lincoln reached the top, Valerie put her hand out for him to grab. He did, and a moment later he was back on the roof. He and Valerie leaned against the building's edge. The silence and majesty of the night once again prevailed. No one said anything initially, but L broke the silence.

"I got her caught," he said in a whisper.

Missy and Valerie shook their heads.

"No, you didn't," Valerie said. "You tried to do what you could."

"It wasn't enough."

"I'm sorry," Valerie offered.

L stepped forward and kicked his foot against the half-wall surrounding the roof. "Sorry doesn't get her back!" he shouted, frustrated.

"That's right," Valerie responded. Then she leaned in to L. "So what will get her back? Running from God, is that it?"

Missy's eyes opened wide as her mouth dropped.

Valerie knew that having such forceful, heated words coming from her own mouth was a rarity. Usually it was Missy who issued the challenges...Valerie was the encourager. *Well,* Valerie thought, *maybe I've learned something from Missy.*

"Get off my case!" L shouted back. "If God cared, why didn't He stop this from happening?! He has the power, doesn't He?! Why do people have to have trouble if God is in control?! Why do people have to die?!"

"Grow up, Lincoln!" Valerie shouted, standing straight up and pointing at him. "Take some responsibility, would you?!

You can't blame everything on God! You're forgetting one very important thing: 1 John 4:8—'God is love.'"

Lincoln folded his arms across his chest.

"That's right, L," Valerie continued. "He is Love. He loves you, and He loves your mom and He loves your dad…"

"Then why did my dad die?!" Lincoln stood up and stormed past Valerie.

"There's a devil out there, L!" Valerie proclaimed, stopping L in his tracks. He faced her as she said, "1 Peter 5:8 says he's walking the streets like a roaring lion, just looking for *someone* to devour. And there's sin in the world. You heard about sin?! Sin, sickness, disease—they're out there steamrolling over the world and threatening believers. We have to stand against all that! We have to stay in God's Word, stay in prayer and speak His promises for health, healing and protection over our lives. You may have lost a battle, L, but God wants you to win the war! It's up to you whether you'll put forth the effort to win in this world or completely give up!"

Lincoln swung away from Valerie, folding his arms across his chest. Valerie threw her hands up in the air. *What more can I say?* she wondered. *Holy Spirit, give him understanding.* Valerie leaned back against the building's edge again.

Lincoln looked down at his bare foot. His shoe sole was hanging off to the side now, dangling like a cat's toy on the end of a string. He swung his foot in the air, angrily trying to snap the sole off the shoe. Finally, it tore away and skidded across the snow-peppered roof. L dropped down, right in a pile of snow and sat cross-legged. His back was to Valerie, and he rubbed his foot with his hand.

Valerie prayed in the spirit, not quite sure what to pray herself.

A long, tense moment passed. L's voice was rough as he quietly said, "It's me, isn't it?"

The soft question cooled Valerie down. She pressed her eyes with her fingers. "What?" she asked.

"The young man in that painting—the prodigal son. That's me, isn't it?"

Valerie's head popped up when the question he asked truly hit her. There he was, rubbing his bare foot, his back to her. Valerie remembered how in Rembrandt's painting, the prodigal son's foot was also exposed from the wear and tear of the world. She remembered how L had rolled his finger on the boy's foot in the painting. Now the sole he touched was his own.

A tear dropped from Valerie's eye before she could catch it. She cleared her throat and said, "The prodigal son is each of us at one point or another."

L nodded. "You're right."

"I am?" Valerie asked, not doubting the truth in her words, but rather L's acceptance of them.

Lincoln nodded. "Yeah," he admitted, "I'm not taking any responsibility. And because of it, I've begun to think everything is hopeless.... And it *is* hopeless without God in my life."

"God is waiting for you to come back to him," Valerie said. "His arms are wide open. He's been watching you every step of the way, just waiting for you to turn around and see Him."

L whispered, "You sure it's not too hard to go back to Him?"

"It's not hard at all. He loves you and He's waiting to hear from you," Valerie said, placing a hand on L's back. "Jesus is our hope of glory," she added, thinking of Colossians 1:27. "If you return to Him, you'll get your hope back...and then you'll have something for your faith to stand on. You'll find it much easier to believe that we'll find your mother."

L stood up, walked a few paces and stared up into the sky. Valerie couldn't see his face, but she could hear him pray. She thought his words were some of the sweetest she had ever heard.

"Father," he prayed simply, "Valerie says You're watching and I guess I should believe her because it seems like something You'd do. You know I've messed up. My whole family has messed up. But we need You. Father God, I want You back in my life. I won't run away again just because something doesn't make sense to me. Next time I will listen to Your Spirit for help. I love You, God. In Jesus' Name, amen."

He turned back around and Valerie looked away like she hadn't been listening so intently to his prayer. Lincoln smiled. "It's all right," he said. "Everything's all right now."

The 11-year-old gave each of the Superkids and Ralph a hug. He even hugged Snicker.

"Well," Missy piped up, forcing the emotion to pass, "everything's all right except that your mom's been captured by raiders, you don't have a home and Ralph keeps calling me 'Nadine.'"

Valerie giggled.

Missy pointed at her. "And I don't want to hear another word from you, Miss Attitude. I never knew you had it in you."

"I'm just full of surprises," Valerie said.

Valerie walked over to the edge of the building again and looked down at the street where Elly was captured.

"Ralph," she addressed the old man, "what was it you said about the raiders?"

He thought for a moment, then his face lit up. "They always

come for the weakest."

Valerie walked over and picked up Snicker. She rubbed his head as she thought.

"The Bible says the Lord 'gives strength to the weary and increases the power of the weak,'" she quoted Isaiah 40:29.

"So..." L pressed.

"So," Valerie continued with a smile, "I think it's about time we proved it. What do you say we lend the raiders a hand?"

Missy leaned forward. "You want to lend the *raiders* a hand?"

Valerie nodded. "You bet I do."

Evening turned to night, and the streets turned to silence. With the intrusion of the raiders, the homeless hid themselves within the nooks and crannies of the city, eager to see the light of the next day.

Valerie, Lincoln, Missy, Ralph and Snicker were scoping out the vacant downtown area, hoping for some signs of life. They hadn't yet seen the whites of anyone's eyes, nor heard a whispered "Run!" to warn them that the raiders were coming.

"This is hopeless," L finally said, frustrated. "We've been walking for nearly two hours and still haven't found anyone. Maybe we should just give up."

"No," Valerie immediately countered. "The Holy Spirit will guide us according to John 16:13. He will show us the way."

"Hey, Val," Missy prompted, "can we stop for a sec? My toes are freezing."

Valerie stopped walking and nodded. Even Snicker, back in L's backpack, was shivering. Valerie pointed up the way. "I see a fire up ahead. Let's go there and warm up before we continue."

Everyone mumbled their agreement and trudged forward, a little faster with the hope of warmth ahead. As they drew closer, they were pleased to see it was what they thought: a trash can with a roaring fire inside. When they finally arrived, Valerie held out her hands and felt the heat burn at her chilled fingers. She closed her eyes for a moment. The others joined her.

After a bit, Missy said, "You know, this is a little strange. This is the first fire we've seen tonight. All the others had practically died out since news of the raid. But this one looks like it was recently set."

Valerie's eyes shot open as a chill ran down her spine. Missy was correct. Something about this wasn't right—a blazing fire on a cold night with no one around it? Valerie slowly turned her head to look around...but the streets were black. Maybe it was nothing.

"You all remember our plan?" she asked. Each member of the team nodded. "Good," she continued. "Look, I think maybe we'd better..."

Run...

Valerie froze. The others froze. They had all heard it. Like a whisper...

Run...

Like a warning...

Run!

Like an alarm...

RUN!!!

The black hovertruck slid in like a shadow. The adventurers barely had time to react when the back hatch popped open.

"It's a trap!" Missy cried, already breaking into a sprint. Lincoln was behind her, not wasting any time. Ralph looked confused and Valerie grabbed his rough hand.

"C'mon!" she shouted. Valerie ran forward, heading directly for the nearest shadow. At the edge of a building, she found a stairwell leading down, beneath the surface of the street.

Hurriedly she pulled Ralph down the steps with her. At the bottom, a huge door blocked their way. Valerie tried it. It was locked tight.

"Stay here," she ordered Ralph. Then she ran up a few steps and looked out into the street. She began praying in the spirit, under her breath. The Holy Spirit, she knew, would know exactly what to pray.

Two black-uniformed soldiers had disembarked the hovertruck and were running after their targets. Missy darted left, then right, then left again, searching for any type of cover. Lincoln had made it to a building with several protruding bricks. He scrambled to climb them and escape the attackers.

Then the first shot was fired at Missy. It hit her with absolute precision, in the small of her back. The familiar green light rippled around her, then changed to a grid net. Missy hit it hard, screamed and then fell to the ground.

Valerie's prayers came faster. With everything within her, she wanted to dash out and try to rescue Missy, but she knew that wasn't the smartest tactical maneuver. Lincoln, on the other hand, was already heading toward the soldier who had shot her. With full force, he crashed into the soldier's side and knocked him down. The soldier cried out, but not soon enough. L had gotten hold of the hand-held "electric net" device. He stood up quickly and pointed it at the soldier.

"Where's my mom?" he asked.

The soldier grinned menacingly.

FZZZZZZZAPP!

Lincoln was hit from behind by the other soldier, the green net covering him. He fell to the ground, releasing the device he held.

One of the soldiers grabbed L by the neck of his jacket and

Missy by her arm. He began to drag them to the hovertruck.

Valerie dropped back down. Her heart was beating fast and she was running out of options. She didn't like being cornered.

She and Ralph stood in the stairwell, waiting. Ralph started to ask about Nadine, but Valerie shushed him. She was about to sneak up the stairwell and check out the street again when she heard it: *tap...tap...tap.*

Footsteps. Valerie didn't stop praying.

Tap...tap...tap.

She closed her eyes. The sound was coming from right above them. There was nowhere to run. If the soldier looked down, they would be found.

Tap...tap...tap.

He was walking past them!

Tap...tap...tap.

"He's not going to find us!" Valerie whispered to Ralph.

Tap...tap...tap.

Cough.

Valerie turned to Ralph wide-eyed. He had coughed! The footsteps above came back quickly. Valerie looked around for any way to get out fast. She pushed at the door. She pulled at the door. Ralph looked worried.

When she turned around, the soldier was at the top of the stairwell, staring down at her and Ralph. The soldier smiled.

"*Homeless,*" he called them as though it were a curse word.

Suddenly a green flash came straight at them.

For Entertainment's Sake

The smoke in the air was encompassing but thin. When Valerie awoke, the smoke was the first thing she noticed, followed by the orange lighting and the hard floor. The moment she felt the cold steel wrapped around her wrist, she remembered exactly what was happening. Slowly, she sat upright, shaking rebel strands of dark-brown hair out of her face. Generators around the room hummed, sending a minute vibration through Valerie's being. But her attention wasn't really on the power sources, the huge ramp in front of her or the pit beyond.

Instead, Valerie's eyes were riveted on the silent beings all around her. Like passengers waiting for a train that would never come, they were packed between the walls, from one side of the room to the other. Men and women sat and lay, waiting. Just waiting. They were the weak, the homeless, dressed in rags, bathed in hopelessness. They sat bound and captured against their will. The only consolation Valerie perceived was that at least they were warm. They all wore handcuffs, electronically locked and controlled by a transmitter.

Valerie turned around and saw Missy lying on the ground near her. She whispered to her, "Missy! *Pssst!* Missy!"

The blond Superkid blinked away the darkness and pulled herself up quickly, disoriented.

"It's all right!" Valerie whispered. "Missy—I'm here."

Missy crinkled her forehead, smiled weakly at Valerie

and took in the room. She cleared her throat and asked, "Where is here?"

Valerie shrugged her shoulders. She wanted to know the answer to that question herself.

About 20 feet away, Lincoln sat up in the crowd and looked around. He spotted Valerie and Missy and motioned to them. Clumsily, he maneuvered himself to his feet and walked over. He sat down, his hands also clasped together behind his back.

"What's going on?" he asked them. This time both the Superkids shrugged their shoulders. "You seen my mom?" he inquired.

Valerie shook her head. "We just woke up ourselves."

L looked around the room. His eyes grew wide when he saw her. "There she is! Mom!" he shouted.

His mother turned and saw him, a smile breaking on her face. "Lincoln!" she shouted.

A buzzing noise like a fire alarm burst through the room and L froze in place. Valerie noticed how the captured people shrunk back in fear. Missy looked at her with an imaginary question mark written on her face. A side door marked with yellow and black stripes slid open and a uniformed soldier entered. Valerie's mouth went dry when she saw the short, three-letter emblem blazoned on his shirt: NME. Suddenly, the evil, the treachery and the trouble made a lot more sense. It was caused by the one organization consistently capable of it: NME, Superkid Academy's enemy. Now Valerie just wanted to know *why*.

"Time for our next test!" the NME agent announced, clapping his hands. "Who would like to be next?"

L never took his eyes off his mother.

Full of the Holy Spirit and boldness, Valerie stood up, quickly regained her balance, and confronted the NME agent.

"I want to know what's going on here!" she demanded, her arms still bound behind her back. "By the Spirit of God, I'm here to tell you to let these people go!"

The guard sneered. "Well, hello, Moses," he said and then snickered. Underneath the NME agent suit, the 20-something man looked like any of hundreds of other agents. But the sneer gave him sudden, distinct personality.

"Such boldness from homeless scum," he said pompously.

Valerie just glared at him. "I want to know what's going on," she stated plainly. To her surprise, the agent put down his guard.

"I'd be happy to fill you in," he said, "on one of NME's greatest achievements."

Oh, now, Valerie thought, *this is going to be good.*

Missy stood and joined her by her side.

The agent walked up the steel ramp slowly, creating his own, dominant atmosphere in the room. The homeless watched silently in fear as each step clicked and echoed eerily. Some of the people whispered, most were stone silent.

Once at the top of the ramp, the NME agent punched a series of buttons on a wall console. Valerie swallowed hard, her own eyes squinting, as she watched the room's captives shrink back. The women's eyes filled with tears, the men's eyes filled with terror. They had seen this before.

At the ramp's edge, on the inside, the metal floor split with a loud hiss. Black smoke billowed out in a puff like a storm cloud, and then dissipated just as fast. The guard looked down in the pit curiously, but then turned his attention back to Valerie, Missy and L.

"While people like you beg and lie around for a living, here at NME we've kept busy. Our goal is to make society better. Using mechanics and holographic breakthroughs, we've been able to create intensive, holo-real environments. In just a small space like this room, we can create as much as a mile's worth of virtual reality in all directions."

Valerie noticed Missy was shaking her head.

"In simpler words," the agent offered, "we have created the perfect jail. The criminal can be kept in a tiny room—while all the while he thinks he's in another world."

"A world of your choosing," Valerie suggested, remembering that she had heard something about this earlier, on the TV in the diner.

"Exactly," the agent punctuated. "Of course, that leaves room for great entertainment value, too. We can put criminals in another time period...say, when knights and castles and fair maidens ruled the land."

"What's the catch?" Missy wondered aloud.

"The catch is that with mechanics and holograms, we can create a little fun: dragons, for instance. They may have never existed...but they do now in our little world. You haven't seen anything until you've seen a man fight a dragon."

"So why kidnap the homeless?" Valerie demanded. She was getting weary of the pompous lecture.

"Well, we have to test the project *somehow,*" he said, belittling Valerie's question. "Our goal is a larger simulation, one the size of an entire building! But some parts—like the dragon, for instance—still need to be tested on actual individuals. And we figure if one of these gets hurt, who cares? No one's going to miss them."

"The Lord cares!" Valerie shouted. She could hardly fathom

what she was hearing. "In Matthew 10:29, the Bible says He cares if even a sparrow falls! How much more does He care for one of us?!"

"Give me a break, kid," the man scolded, "you're starting to sound like a Superkid. These here"—he said sweeping his arms out to the hungry, cowering men and women—"are different. Look at them! Look at you! We're doing the world a favor by using you in our tests. We're ridding the world of sickness!"

The words stung Valerie. *How could anyone truly think that?*

Missy's mouth suddenly dropped and she staggered back like someone had just socked her in the stomach.

"Missy, what's wrong?" Valerie asked.

"I said that," she responded in a whisper. Valerie stared at her for a long moment. Missy was right—she had said the same thing: "I'm not like *them.* They're not as health-conscious as me."

"So we're sick?" L had asked. Missy had responded with, "Well, yeah…only in a manner of speaking." She said it when they first showed up at the Geofferson Mission.

"Missy, now's not the time…"

"I'm no different from him," Missy said, her eyes watering up.

"Missy, he's an NME agent!" Valerie contradicted. "You *are* different."

"No!" Missy shouted. "I mean I'm no different on the inside!"

"But you're a Christian!"

"Then why am I like this?!" Missy cried, struggling with her hands behind her back.

"We're all working through things," Valerie consoled. "The difference between you and him is that you are listening to the Holy Spirit convicting your heart. You see that it's wrong…and you want to make it right."

"But I haven't made it right!" Missy admitted. "This isn't just about him," she said, angling her head at the NME agent. "It's about Mashela, too. You remember what I went through with Mashela? I forgave her...but my sin was pride. I was always looking down on her. And I'm still looking down on people. I haven't changed."

Valerie bit her lip. Mashela Knavery was another NME agent who Missy had confronted only a few weeks earlier. For the longest time, Missy had looked down on Mashela, thinking she was better than the NME agent. Then she realized Mashela was a person, too...a person in need of a Savior.

But now Missy had come full circle. She thought she had gotten rid of those feelings of pride and superiority...but perhaps not entirely. "I'm so sorry," Missy said, slowly looking around the room. "I'm so sorry."

Missy's eyes suddenly stopped tearing and they grew wide in surprise. Valerie followed her line of sight. The NME agent had pulled a coughing, homeless man from the crowd and was leading him up the ramp at gunpoint. It was Ralph.

Valerie gasped. "What are you doing?!" she shouted.

"I told you," the agent said nonchalantly, "it's time for another test." He continued up the ramp.

"No!" Missy hopped over a woman reclined in front of her and ran up the ramp. The agent whirled his weapon around and pointed it at her. She froze.

"Take me instead," she pleaded. "He's of no use to you. I'll be a better test victim against..." Missy nodded her head dubiously at the pit. "...whatever you've got down there."

"It's a whole other world down there," the NME agent said proudly.

Ralph looked worried. "Nadine..." he whimpered.

"No!" Valerie shouted, running forward. She addressed Missy. "Ralph needs you." Then she looked at the NME agent. "Take me."

The agent grabbed her arm forcefully and laughed. "This is the first time there has been so much interest in going down there," he said. "Fine!" He waved his laser pistol in the air. "You two, get away!" he shouted louder than necessary at Missy and Ralph. Valerie saw L standing between herself and his mother, not sure what to do.

As Valerie walked the rest of the way up the ramp, it seemed steeper than it looked. She felt the weight of gravity pulling her backward, coaxing her to turn and run as fast as she could. But she wouldn't. She couldn't.

A strong smell of sulfur came from the opening in the floor. Valerie winced. "What's down there?" she asked.

From behind her, the NME agent typed her cuff number into a small, silver transmitter dangling from a key chain hooked to his belt loop. Her handcuffs fell off. The agent kept the gun steady at her back.

"I told you, it's a virtual masterpiece," he said. "Another world. Now climb down." Valerie couldn't see much beyond the opening. At her feet, though, was a rope ladder, tied to two loops in the steel floor. Valerie placed one foot back and balanced it on the first rope rung.

"Go!" the agent ordered, his eyes wild.

"There's one down there, isn't there?" Valerie asked calmly, to her own surprise.

"You mean a dragon?" the agent questioned. "Perhaps," he answered, smiling. "Maybe you'll even get a second to see a perfectly created medieval environment."

Valerie swallowed hard. She could feel the perspiration forming on her forehead and hands. She stepped down another rung, holding on to the ladder with her right hand. The rope strands pricked her hand. She stepped down another rung. Halfway down the ladder, when the agent's gun was at eye level, she stopped.

From below, she heard a growling sound.

"Even though I walk through the valley of the shadow of death, I will fear no evil, for you are with me," Valerie spoke from Psalm 23. It was a verse her mother had always spoken to her when she was a child.

The agent shoved his weapon under Valerie's chin, forcing her face up.

"Get down there!" he ordered.

Valerie shook her head.

"I have to tell you something," Valerie said to the guard.

Impatient, he tilted his head as if to ask, *"What now?"*

"We've given you a good performance," Valerie continued.

"What do you mean?"

"What I mean is that we figured you'd capture us if you thought we were weak, and we were right. That wisdom was our strength."

"Shut up and get down there!"

Another growl resounded in the chamber below.

Valerie winked at the guard and then looked across to L in the crowd beyond.

Then she nodded.

The nod was the cue. Lincoln doubled over and his back-pack flipped open over his head. Like a bullet out of a shot-gun, Snicker barked and launched from the backpack, heading straight up the ramp. The NME agent turned in surprise as the mutt came straight at him. Heading for the shiniest item in the room, the dog bounced up like a clown on a trampoline and set its jaw around the silver transmitter on the key chain tied to the agent's belt loop. With all his force, the dog tore the belt loop and snatched its prize away.

No sooner was Snicker heading down the ramp than the agent aimed at the dog with his gun. But Valerie reacted quickly. A third hand mysteriously popped out of her raggedy jacket and clamped around the gun.

FZZZZZZZAPP!

A laser shot went off, blowing a hole in the wall across the room.

At the bottom of the ramp, L and Missy popped third hands out from behind their shabby clothes, too. The jailer dropped his jaw in wonderment. Valerie saw the shock roll across his face as he realized they had outsmarted him: Each of them had attached a false hand to their left sleeve. He had actually only handcuffed each of their right hands to a false hand. Their *real* left hands were hidden beneath their clothing all along.

"Give a helping hand!" Missy shouted with a wide smile,

quoting the Geofferson Mission bulletin board where they had retrieved the fake appendages before wandering the streets, waiting to be captured by the hovertruck.

Missy grabbed the transmitter from Snicker and began to free the homeless, one by one. As she did, cries of freedom and joy went up around the room. Lincoln ran to his mother, throwing his arms around her.

The guard spun back around and focused his attention on the tug of war with the gun.

"You can't put your trust in the weapons of this world!" Valerie shouted as she pulled the gun away from him. The agent lurched forward angrily. Valerie fought to keep her balance, but with the pit behind her, it was all she could do to stay on the ladder.

Valerie threw the gun behind her as hard as she could, hoping it would fall into the pit. Instead, it clanked against a bar and landed on the far corner of the opening. The agent shot forward for the gun again.

Valerie was knocked back this time and her fingers lost their grip on the rope. She felt herself being tossed backward and down into the unknown holographic world below.

Snag!

The Superkid's foot caught the end of the rope! Dangling upside down, Valerie knocked her jacket and fake hand off. They dropped—and Valerie watched them fall at least 100 feet...a fall she didn't want to take herself.

That's when she noticed the foliage around her. Lush greens and browns, not unlike the colors of her home on Calypso Island. But these greens and browns were thicker trees than she was used to: These were oaks, ashes and redwoods. It seemed impossible—a complete forest holographically created beneath the warehouse.

Above she saw the NME agent finally reach his gun. He stood on the edge and laughed, looking down at her. He aimed his weapon. Then he thought twice and aimed at the ladder. He shot at one of the tied knots.

FZZZZZZZAPP!

Valerie screamed. One side of the ladder tore away as the laser burned through the rope knot. Valerie swung down farther, dangling like a monkey on a thin tree branch.

Then the trees rustled.

The atmosphere filled with smoke.

The air smelled of sulfur.

A deep, throaty, gurgling sound resounded around her.

The NME agent above laughed and ran away from the pit. He apparently didn't think it was necessary to take out the other knot. He obviously knew something she didn't.

Valerie's leg began to tingle.

"God, my hope is in You," she prayed aloud. "You are my strength and shield. Psalm 28:7 says it. And I will not be harmed, in Jesus' Name!"

Valerie mustered together any strength she had left and lifted her body up to meet the rope. She grabbed on to a rung and tried to steady herself as the ladder twirled in the air like a pinwheel in the wind.

She pulled herself up a rung. Suddenly a series of tree branches broke and hot air hit her legs. *Very* hot air. She looked down and couldn't believe it when she saw it: It looked real. It looked alive. It spied her with its catlike, red eyes. *A dragon.*

Just like out of the picture books, NME had created a

holographic dragon that looked and acted as though it were the real thing, if there had ever been one. Its nostrils flared, its pupils dilated, its eyelids tightened, its brown and green scales rippled around its jaw in hunger and in anger.

"It's not real," she kept telling herself. "That monster is not real!" She turned her back on it and continued to rise.

The dragon roared like a lion, only louder—much louder. Smoke poured out of its nose and to Valerie's surprise, fire came out of its mouth—straight at her.

Valerie leapt up a rung, inwardly thanking God for the strength she had requested. Her heart was pounding like the beat of a bumblebee's wings. The dragon pulled away, giving Valerie only a moment to breathe.

Suddenly she realized her feet still felt very hot. The ladder was on fire!

From the bottom up, the fire licked Valerie's feet like a snake's tongue, flickering up and back, gaining ground as it rose.

Valerie scrambled up as fast as she could.

With the fire at her heels, Valerie flipped up over the top of the opening to the pit faster than she thought possible. A plume of fire billowed out of the hole. The next thing she knew, she was beside the NME agent's feet, hot but safe. He was standing in front of her, but wasn't paying any attention to her. He was facing out...and he had someone in his arms.

"STOP!" the NME agent ordered. Valerie watched the room freeze, like a movie paused in the middle of a crucial scene. The homeless men and women who had been hugging and rubbing their sore wrists didn't move a muscle.

The agent had hold of a familiar-looking figure. And L's

expression confirmed who it was, though Valerie couldn't see her face. It was Lincoln's mother, Elly. The NME agent had her. *This* wasn't part of the plan.

"Mom!" L shouted, his chin quivering. He didn't move, didn't risk the agent using his weapon.

The NME agent mercilessly jerked her head back by her hair and shoved his gun under her neck. Snicker barked. Missy and Ralph stood together, the transmitter that had freed so many captives, dangling from the key chain in Missy's hand.

Valerie wanted so badly to go back in time, just five minutes. Just long enough to change her actions. Perhaps she could have scrambled up the ladder faster. Perhaps she could have thrown the agent's gun more precisely, causing it to bounce into the dragon's lair. Perhaps she could have planned better. Perhaps...

Since the beginning of the mission, everything seemed to be out of control. Like a rubber band, Valerie felt herself stretching, hoping that one day everything would be back to normal. But right now, right here, lying on the ground, there was nothing she could do.

"Drop the transmitter!" the agent shouted at Missy. She quickly complied, dropping it on the ground.

"Let her go!" L cried. Valerie saw the side of Elly's face. L's mother was trying to smile, but she was too weak. She looked malnourished...and like she had suffered a beating. Her round face was pale and worn, scarred by the months on the street.

"You're all going to do what I say or every one of you will go into the pit!" the agent taunted. Veins popped out on his neck like thick cords running from his jaw line to his chest.

"Everyone over there!" the madman urged with a wave of his weapon. Slowly, the homeless men and women began to shuffle to a single side of the room. But one did not shuffle. One did not move. Lincoln held his ground.

"Move!" the NME agent ordered.

L's face became as flint. His body tensed. "I have something to say," he boldly stated. The words flowed naturally: "Mom, I love you."

Elly bit her lip. Even to Valerie the words were pleasant and encouraging, like the light of a tiny match seen at the end of a deep, dark passageway.

Elly forced out the words, "I love you, too, L." Her voice cracked.

Lincoln stayed stiff as he replied, "We're going to make it through this, Mom. I've got hope: Even though we gave up on Him, God hasn't given up on us."

"Shuddup!" the agent shouted. "It's hopeless for you now! MOVE!"

Lincoln stood his ground. "My hope is on the solid rock of Jesus," he replied to the agent, "and my faith is built on that hope. God has changed me...and there isn't any shaking that faith."

"We'll see," the agent spat. He raised his laser gun and pointed it straight at L, who still refused to move. His finger slowly placed pressure on the trigger as he aimed.

FZZZZZZZAPP-POW!

L staggered back and reached for his chest, but whirled around when he heard the wall burning behind and above him. The agent had missed. L flinched and turned around to see the reason: Elly's elbow was buried deep in the NME agent's stomach. With full force, she had come back with her arm and plunged it into her captor. The agent stepped back as he let out an "ooofff," but Valerie didn't have enough time to move. The

NME agent tripped over her and went straight back into the pit.

He screamed loudly in fright, reminding Valerie of what a boar on Calypso Island sounds like when it first steps into a trap.

Valerie quickly shifted her body backward and sideways. She reached out to grab the agent from the certain death below. She managed to grab a clump of his coat just as he was dropping down. The force of his fall jerked her forward. She would have gone in with him if it wasn't for Elly landing on her legs and holding her.

The NME agent stared upward in fright and reached up to grab Valerie's hand. Below, the warning of a deep growl sounded. The fog covering the sight below blew away with the hot breath of the dragon.

The agent shrieked in terror. His hand was tightly clasped around Valerie's, but it wasn't enough of a grip. Valerie couldn't pull him up.

"What happened?!" the agent cried.

"You underestimated the power of hope," Valerie said pointedly, straining to keep hold. "The power it delivers gives strength to even the weakest captive."

"Pull me up!" he whimpered. Valerie saw shades of green and brown arise from beneath him.

Valerie could feel the strain on her hand. She couldn't hold him much longer.

Suddenly Valerie felt heat on the back of her hand. It was coming from the burning ladder. It was burning hot, and in a moment it would singe her skin. It would force her to let go.

The dragon below roared, sending a tremor through the floor.

Valerie held on as long as she could.

The agent's hand was being pulled out of hers by the force of gravity. Her hand was bright red from the fire.

She couldn't...hold on...much...

Suddenly another hand appeared, slid past Valerie's, and grabbed tight on to the NME agent. Valerie knew by the red fingernail polish to whom it belonged. The agent looked up in absolute surprise and found himself speechless. Valerie let go and repositioned her hand, away from the burning rope.

Missy looked down at the agent and spoke firmly. "You know, not everything we've done here was part of a performance."

The agent looked at her, wondering what she was talking about.

"I actually realized something," she told the hanging NME guard. "What you said was right. The difference between you and the homeless *is* sickness."

"It is?!"

"Yes," Missy offered, "but the homeless aren't the ones who are sick. The way I see it, pride is the worst sickness of all."

The agent looked at her curiously. Valerie and Missy pulled as the dragon below blew hot air and smoke at the agent. The dragon snapped at his backside, tearing his trousers. "Yow!" It gave Valerie and Missy the momentum they needed to raise him up. Moments later they had him on top of the ramp again. For a few moments the agent breathed heavily, then rose and stumbled back down the ramp. He took one last look at Valerie and Missy lying at the opening and harshly whispered, "Useless." Then he took off out a side door.

Missy glanced over to Valerie. "How's that for gratitude?" But Valerie wasn't listening. Her eyes were fixed on the young boy and his mother, arm in arm, with a dog joyfully bouncing at their feet.

Standing up weakly, Missy walked down the ramp, picked up the transmitter and began to finish her job of freeing the prisoners. Valerie peeked down into the pit once more and then punched a couple of buttons on the side panel, closing it tight. She didn't care to confront the fake dragon. For now, she would leave that for a future mission.

Casually and thoughtfully, Valerie walked down to the mother and son. She wasn't trying to listen in to their shared words, but she couldn't help overhearing. Elly was explaining to L why she left...and Valerie could tell by the tone in her voice, she wasn't proud of her actions.

"I lost my job that night," Elly said sadly, "and it was more than I could take. I never should have left, but I lost all hope...I didn't know what else to do."

"I missed you so much," L cried as she stroked his hair. "I thought I might never see you again."

"I just kept planning on coming back when things got better, so I could raise you right, but they never did...I know it was so wrong...I know...I know...I promise to never leave you again. Please forgive me, L."

"I forgive you, Mom," L said, his face buried in her neck. "I gave up on God, too. I'm just glad I found you, even if I didn't deserve to..."

"Oh, L, I don't deserve to have you," she said.

Valerie felt compassion rise up in her spirit like a flood of water pressing to break through a dam. She walked over and placed a caring hand on each of their backs. She caught L's eye and smiled.

"God doesn't treat you like NME," she offered. "You may not deserve it, but He'll show you mercy anyway."

L took in a deep breath and smiled, too. "Just like the father in the story of the prodigal son."

"Exactly," Valerie confirmed. "Now let's give Missy some help and get out of here. This place will be crawling with NME guards in no time."

Seventeen hours later, Geofferson Mission was at full capacity. Reverend Michael Bankson was welcoming in the droves and greeting each homeless person with a smile. The personal warmth broke the chill vying to get through the door.

At the bulletin board, Valerie was tying the false hands back up, returning the display to its previous state. Beside her, Lincoln helped, though he took a brief break at one point to dust the frame around Rembrandt's *The Return of the Prodigal Son.* Valerie wondered if Rembrandt, like L, ever saw himself as the prodigal son in that picture.

The door to the chapel was partially blocked by Missy and Ralph. She was shaking his hand and saying goodbye.

"Thank you for all your help," she said.

Ralph nodded.

"Now, I don't want you to go out on that street again, you hear me? You need to get over this cold of yours. Reverend Bankson said he'll be able to keep you busy with washing the dishes and helping out in the kitchen. But you have to stay faithful. It's a good job."

Ralph was still nodding, and a smile popped up on his face. Suddenly Ralph reached forward and gave Missy a big, bear hug. At first she yelped from surprise, but she gave in and hugged Ralph back—a sight Valerie was pleased to see. When he pulled away, the old man with whiskers whispered, "I love you, Nadine."

Missy bit her lip. "I love you, too, Ralph," she said kindly. As Ralph retreated into the chapel, Missy watched until he was comfortably seated.

"I'm gonna miss him," she admitted.

L chuckled. "Now *there's* something I never thought I'd hear you say."

Missy messed up L's hair. "Val's not the only one full of surprises," she replied, shooting a wink at Valerie.

Valerie pinned up the final appendage and stepped back to look at her work. Pleased with her job well done, Valerie walked down the hall to see how Elly was doing.

Lincoln's mother was applying a touch of antibiotic and a bandage around a homeless man's finger. He winced like a baby dreading medicine.

"How's it going on the first night of your new employment?" Valerie asked politely.

Elly patted the taped bandage and smiled at the man. He thanked her and stepped away. She brushed a strand of her black hair behind her ear and scooted over a tad. Valerie joined her on the bench.

"I want to thank you again," Elly said. "This is just what Lincoln and I needed right now."

"Well, from the moment I saw that memo on the bulletin board about the reverend needing medical help for the mission, I had you in mind. I just thank God we found you safe and sound."

"I couldn't have asked for more," Elly elaborated. "We now have room and board in exchange for our help, Lincoln can go back to school, and we'll have enough extra to live on. God really supplied our needs, Valerie."

"He does that," Valerie said. "And as you are faithful in your giving, you'll see a plentiful harvest over time. I guarantee it."

"I'm glad Reverend Bankson said he's going to get me involved with a church group that can help me, too," Elly admitted. "I just don't want to fail again."

"Don't look at it as a failure," Valerie said. "See it as a learning step. Work at it. Determine to get God's hope deep inside you. Then your faith has something to build on. It'll pay off if you don't give up."

As Elly hugged her, the thought occurred to Valerie that she was also preaching to herself. For someone who always liked being in control, this mission taught her that sometimes she just needed to trust that God knew what He was doing. In the end, everything worked according to His plan. Even in such a messed up, runaway mission, everything was finally back in a state of order.

"Hey!" L shouted from down the hall. "Has anyone seen Snicker?"

The Superkids, Elly and Reverend Bankson all looked at each other in curiosity. *Come to think of it,* Valerie thought, *I haven't seen that dog since we returned.*

"Maybe I shouldn't have given you permission to let him run around the shelter," Reverend Bankson kidded.

"You know, I wonder..." Lincoln said, trailing off as he walked down the hall to the room where he used to hide Snicker. The door was ajar.

L peeked in and his eyes grew wide. He quickly shut the door.

"Uh-oh," he said, gulping.

"What?" his mother asked cautiously. The group gathered

around the door and slowly L pushed it open again.

There, in the center of the small room, lay Snicker beside a high pile of treasures—forks, spoons, watches, pens—anything that shined. The mutt tilted his head as if to ask, "May I help you?"

Valerie's mouth dropped. "He gathered all that himself?"

"He really does like shiny objects, doesn't he?" Missy added.

The reverend started to chuckle. Missy let out a giggle. Elly smiled, covering her face and shaking her head. Lincoln, too, began to laugh. And Valerie couldn't help but join in.

So, not *everything* was in order yet. To Valerie, that wasn't such a dreaded thought anymore. Because it proved to her—beyond a shadow of a doubt—that with God on her side, she could always look forward to the hope of an interesting tomorrow.

At the same moment Valerie and Missy had vanished during their mission briefing, Alex had disappeared too. But he didn't find himself under a pile of snow or sitting in a pew. He found himself in a closet.

He jiggled the knob, kicked the door and shouted for help, but no one came. Several hours later, he heard voices. He almost shouted again, but then he heard what they were saying...

"Yes, sir," the first voice said. "Commander Kellie just answered our call for help. Didn't take long."

"I knew she'd answer," a second voice replied. "Her weakness is her love for people."

I recognize those voices, Alex thought. *But from where?*

There was some rustling, then the first voice said, "So here's the latest blueprint. Notice the positions of the holocams. It's technological brilliance. We can create a multidimensional layout that changes the landscape as you move. You could think you've run five miles, but in reality, you haven't moved but an inch."

"We got what we paid for," said the second voice. "So how are the mechanics?"

The first voice snickered. "We've been testing them on the homeless and they work perfectly. Soon we can imprison anyone in a world full of death and destruction."

"Perfect." Then, "I can't wait until Commander Kellie is ours. She'll never escape."

Alex's eyes grew big.

"The best thing," voice number one noted, "is that no one will even know. It looks like a normal building from the outside, but the inside…"

"Is full of danger," completed voice number two.

Suddenly a communicator rang and a muffled conversation followed. The two men left the room, but not before one walked over to the closet, opened it and threw a tube inside. Alex held his breath, hoping he wouldn't be caught. But they didn't notice him and quickly went on their way.

Having left the closet unlocked, Alex easily exited.

The room was dimly lit—some sort of storage room piled high with nondescript wooden boxes. Alex turned and grabbed the tube the man had thrown into the closet. He popped a plastic lid off one end and reached inside. He pulled out a large, rectangular schematic of a building at 2236 Roland Drive. It was filled with holograms and mechanisms—a real technological wonder. But what really puzzled him were the labels: STABLES, CAVE, DARK CASTLE, LAKE, WELL 1, WELL 2, VILLAGE, DUNGEON A, O.S. LAIR and more. If Alex didn't know better, he'd think someone had created plans for a mammoth, interactive, holographic environment. But creating something like that would be impossible.

Wouldn't it?

Alex blinked and shook his head. The dim storage room was suddenly gone. He was safely back at Superkid Academy, where he belonged. He let out a long breath. Then his thoughts ran together. He found himself in the main Control Room at the Academy. It was empty, except for Paul and Rapper and a few young workers performing routine maintenance. Paul and

Rapper were talking.

"Well, I'm in," Rapper was assuring Paul, punching his shoulder. "I don't care how it happened—I just want to get her back."

"Except we have no *clue* as to where to start! Not to mention that Alex is gone and Missy and Valerie are on another mission."

"Actually *I* know where to start!" said Alex from behind them.

"Alex!" Rapper cried, jumping back.

"Whoa!" Paul shouted. "Where'd you come from?!"

"I've been on a mission myself," Alex answered. He looked around.

"Where's Commander Kellie?" he asked.

Paul looked at Rapper. "That's the bad news. You're not going to believe this, but we left yesterday to answer a call for help and—"

"They got her?" Alex asked. "Already?"

"You know who took her?!" Paul pressed.

Alex shook his head. "No I don't." He held up the blueprints he found. "But I think I know where to find her."

"You do?!" Paul shouted.

"I do. The mission the Lord sent me on led me to *this.*"

The long, beige cylinder of paper was rolled up in Alex's dark fists. Paul and Rapper looked at it in wonder. Alex moved over to the long, purplish, Superkid mission table at the east corner of the control room. He set the cylinder down and unrolled it.

"It looks old," Rapper observed. Paul nodded.

Alex showed Paul and Rapper the crude map within its coils, with the areas labeled: STABLES, CAVE, DARK CASTLE,

LAKE, WELL 1, WELL 2, VILLAGE, DUNGEON A, O.S. LAIR.

Alex paused, "Shouldn't we get Missy and Valerie?"

Paul answered, "They're on another mission. We'll have to go after Commander Kellie alone."

"Well, we can't go like this," Alex said. "I think we're about to enter a holographic world set in medieval times…set *inside* this building." He pointed to the Roland Drive address scrawled down the side of the schematic.

"What? You mean like a video game?"

"More like a time machine," Alex answered. Once you enter the building, you'll *feel* like you've entered another time period.

"So why was Commander Kellie taken there?"

"We won't know unless we go," said Alex. "I'll explain on the way. But let's just say we'd better get some shining armor, men. Because we're about to rescue our commander…as the first Superkid knights!"

To be continued...

The Blue Squad leader is **imprisoned** in a medieval,
holographic adventure...and so are her **rescuers.**

Look for *Commander Kellie and the Superkids*_{SM}
novel #11—

The Knight-Time Rescue
of Commander Kellie

by Christopher P.N. Maselli

Prayer for Salvation

Father God, I believe that Jesus is Your Son and that You raised Him from the dead for me. Jesus, I give my life to You. Right now, I make You the Lord of my life and choose to follow You forever. I love You and I know You love me. Thank You, Jesus, for giving me a new life. Thank You for coming into my heart and being my Savior. I am a child of God! Amen.

About the Author

For more than 10 years, **Christopher P. N. Maselli** has been sharing God's Word with kids through fiction. He is the author of more than 30 books including Zonderkidz' *Laptop* series and the *Superkids* Adventures. He is also the founder of TruthPop.com, dedicated to reaching tweens with the Truth through pop culture.

A graduate of Oral Roberts University, Chris lives in Fort Worth, Texas, with his wife, Gena. He is actively involved in his church's *KIDS Church* program, and his hobbies include inline skating, collecting *It's a Wonderful Life* movie memorabilia and "way too much" computing.

World Offices
of Kenneth Copeland Ministries

For more information about KCM and a free
catalog, please write the office nearest you:

Kenneth Copeland Ministries
Fort Worth, Texas 76192-0001

Kenneth Copeland
Locked Bag 2600
Mansfield Delivery Centre
QUEENSLAND 4122
AUSTRALIA

Kenneth Copeland
Private Bag X 909
FONTAINEBLEAU
2032
REPUBLIC OF
SOUTH AFRICA

Kenneth Copeland Ministries
Post Office Box 84
L'VIV 79000
UKRAINE

Kenneth Copeland
Post Office Box 15
BATH
BA1 3XN
U.K.

Kenneth Copeland
Post Office Box 378
Surrey, B.C.
V3T 5B6
CANADA

We're Here for You!

Believer's Voice of Victory **Television Broadcast**

Join Kenneth and Gloria Copeland and the *Believer's Voice of Victory* broadcasts Monday through Friday and on Sunday each week, and learn how faith in God's Word can take your life from ordinary to extraordinary. This teaching from God's Word is designed to get you where you want to be—*on top!*

You can catch the *Believer's Voice of Victory* broadcast on your local, cable or satellite channels.

Check your local listings for times and stations in your area.

Believer's Voice of Victory **Magazine**

Enjoy inspired teaching and encouragement from Kenneth and Gloria Copeland and guest ministers each month in the *Believer's Voice of Victory* magazine. Also included are real-life testimonies of God's miraculous power and divine intervention in the lives of people just like you!

It's more than just a magazine—it's a ministry.

To receive a FREE subscription to *Believer's Voice of Victory,* write to:

Kenneth Copeland Ministries
Fort Worth, Texas 76192-0001
Or call:
1-800-600-7395
(7 a.m.-5 p.m. CT)
Or visit our Web site at:
www.kcm.org

If you are writing from outside the U.S., please contact the KCM office nearest you. Addresses for all Kenneth Copeland Ministries offices are listed on the previous pages.